A LIFE OF ADVENTURE AND DELIGHT

STORIES

AKHIL SHARMA

First published in the UK in 2017 by Faber & Faber Ltd
Bloomsbury House, 74–77 Great Russell Street,
London, WC1B 3DA

This paperback edition first published in 2018

First published in the US in 2017 by W. W. Norton & Company, Inc.
500 Fifth Avenue, New York, N.Y. 10110

Printed and bound by CPI Group (UK) Ltd, Croydon, CR0 4YY

A LIFE OF ADVENTURE AND DELIGHT is a work of fiction. Names, characters, places, and incidents are the products of the author's imagination or are used fictitiously. Any resemblance to actual events, locales, or persons, living or dead, is entirely coincidental.

"Cosmopolitan" was first published in *The Atlantic*. "Surrounded by Sleep," "A Life of Adventure and Delight," "We Didn't Like Him," "A Heart Is Such a Heavy Thing," and "You Are Happy?" were first published in *The New Yorker*. "The Well" was first published in *The Paris Review*. These stories have been revised from their previously published versions.

A CIP record for this book
is available from the British Library

ISBN 978–0–571–32632–7

AND DELIGHT

Akhil Sharma is the author of two novels, *An Obedient Father* and *Family Life*, which won the Folio Prize and the International Dublin Literary Award. He was selected as one of Granta's Best of Young American Novelists and lives in New York.

Further praise for *A Life of Adventure and Delight*:

'[Sharma is] perhaps the most understated, restrained of modern writers, yet also a vital, pure storyteller.' *Sydney Morning Herald*

'Too many writers let a simple-minded, tragic tone dominate their books. Sharma's stories are too clever for that. In their own subtle and emotionally complex way, they capture the sad comedy of ordinary life. Who repeatedly hurt him? What goes on in the mind of the new bride, so quiet as to appear a bit dim, or the child whose mother is an alcoholic? Sharma infiltrates their thoughts and makes them complex, multidimensional and entirely fascinating.' *Herald*

'Eight haunting, revelatory stories . . . Sharma is boldly forthright and probing . . . Sharma's book feels like a cultural exposé and a lacerating critique of a certain type of male ego. Perceptive, humane and pointed.' Adrian Tomine, *New York Times*

'These beautiful, funny, intelligent short stories are told with such apparent simplicity . . . [Sharma's] writing shines its clean light, never mercilessly or voyeuristically, on these characters winding round and round inside the muddied opacity of their lives a is, the stories sound nic too, in the broade nd ironic, not

overwrought. The genius lies in the detail, in the gritty comical solidity of real things.' Tessa Hadley, *Guardian*

'Expectations for Akhil Sharma's new collection of short stories, *A Life of Adventure and Delight*, were high indeed. And he doesn't disappoint, with eight beautifully sleek, minimally written but emotionally shattering tales – dealing with the paradoxes, ironies and harmonies of modern life. A must.' *Sunday Telegraph*

'Sharma's ample talent and focus on technical literary achievement are on full display here . . . Each sentence a clean, measured stroke.' *Financial Times*

'The stories in Akhil Sharma's *A Life of Adventure and Delight* sweep across the page like monsoons – filled with energy, chaos, surprise, and rapture, they ravish and transform the very nature of reading.' Adam Johnson, National Book Award-winning author of *Fortune Smiles*

'One reads Akhil Sharma's stories as one might watch waves approach the shore on which one stands, understanding that something unseen and powerful is driving them. The waves and the stories are beautiful, deceptively simple, and potentially dangerous.' Viet Thanh Nguyen, Pulitzer Prize-winning author of *The Sympathizer*

'Readers wade into these stories as though stepping into a calm river only to be caught by the undercurrent of the most devastating kind – the demand of everyday existence. Akhil Sharma's words touch the deep experience that often remains wordless. He is truly the Chekhov of our time.' Yiyun Li, author of *Dear Friend, from My Life I Write to You in Your Life*

'Akhil Sharma's deceptively simple diction has a way of cutting straight to the human bone. The stories in *A Life of Adventure and Delight* are revelations, every one.' Richard Russo, Pulitzer Prize-winning author of *Empire Falls* and *Everybody's Fool*

ALSO BY AKHIL SHARMA

An Obedient father

Family Life

FOR LISA SWANSON

CONTENTS

A LIFE OF ADVENTURE AND DELIGHT

COSMOPOLITAN

A little after ten in the morning Mrs. Shaw walked across Gopal Maurya's lawn to his house. It was Saturday, and Gopal was asleep on the couch. The house was dark. When he first heard the doorbell, the ringing became part of a dream. Only he had been in the house during the four months since his wife had followed his daughter out of his life, and the sound of the bell joined somehow with his dream to make him feel ridiculous. Mrs. Shaw rang the bell again. Gopal woke confused and anxious, the state he was in most mornings. He was wearing only underwear and socks, but his blanket was cold from sweat.

He stood up and hurried to the door. He looked through the peephole. The sky was bright and clear. Mrs. Shaw was standing sideways about a foot from the door, and appeared to be staring out over his lawn at her house. She was short and red haired and wore a pink sweatshirt and gray jogging pants.

"Hold on! Hold on, Mrs. Shaw!" he shouted, and ran back into the living room to search for a pair of pants and a shirt. The light was dim, and he had difficulty finding them. As he groped under and behind the couch and looked among the clothes crumpled on the floor, he worried that Mrs. Shaw would not wait and was already walking down the steps. He wondered if he had time to turn on the light to make his search easier. This was typical of the details that could baffle him in the morning.

Mrs. Shaw and Gopal had been neighbors for about two years, but Gopal had met her only three or four times in passing. From his wife he had learned that Mrs. Shaw was a guidance counselor at the high school his daughter had attended. He also learned that she had been divorced for a decade. Her husband, a successful orthodontist, had left her. Since then Mrs. Shaw had moved five or six times, though rarely more than a few miles from where she had last lived. She had bought the small mustard-colored house next to Gopal's as part of this restlessness. Although he did not dislike Mrs. Shaw, Gopal was irritated by the peeling paint on her house and the weeds sprouting out of her broken asphalt driveway, as if by association his house were becoming shabbier. The various cars that left her house late at night made him see her as dissolute. But all this Gopal was willing to forget that morning, in exchange for even a minor friendship.

Gopal found the pants and shirt and tugged them on as

he returned to open the door. The light and cold air swept in, reminding him of what he must look like. Gopal was a small man, with delicate high cheekbones and long eyelashes. He had always been proud of his looks and had dressed well. Now he feared that the gray stubble and long hair made him appear bereft.

"Hello, Mr. Maurya," Mrs. Shaw said, looking at him and through him into the darkened house, and then again at him. The sun shone behind her. The sky was blue dissolving into white. "How are you?" she asked gently.

"Oh, Mrs. Shaw," Gopal said, his voice pitted and rough, "some bad things have happened to me." He had not meant to speak so directly. He stepped out of the doorway.

The front door opened into a vestibule, and one had a clear view from there of the living room and the couch where Gopal slept. He switched on the lights. To the right was the kitchen. The round Formica table and the counters were dusty. Mrs. Shaw appeared startled by this detail. After a moment she said, "I heard." She paused and then quickly added, "I am sorry, Mr. Maurya. It must be hard. You must not feel ashamed; it's no fault of yours."

"Please, sit," Gopal said, motioning to a chair next to the kitchen table. He wanted to tangle her in conversation and keep her there for hours. He wanted to tell her how the loneliness had made him fantasize about calling an ambulance so that he could be touched and prodded, or how for a while he had begun loitering at the Indian grocery store like the old men who have not learned English. What a pretty, good woman, he thought.

Mrs. Shaw stood in the center of the room and looked around her. She was slightly overweight, and her nostrils appeared to be perfect circles, but her small white Reebok sneakers made Gopal see her as fleet with youth and innocence. "I've been thinking of coming over. I'm sorry I didn't."

"That's fine, Mrs. Shaw," Gopal said, standing near the phone on the kitchen wall. "What could anyone do? I am glad, though, that you are visiting." He searched for something else to say. To extend their time together, Gopal walked to the refrigerator and asked her if she wanted anything to drink.

"No, thank you," she said.

"Orange juice, apple juice, or grape, pineapple, guava. I also have some tropical punch," he continued, opening the refrigerator door wide, as if to show he was not lying.

"That's all right," Mrs. Shaw said, and they both became quiet. The sunlight pressed through windows that were laminated with dirt. "You must remember, everybody plays a part in these things, not just the one who is left," she said, and then they were silent again. "Do you need anything?"

"No. Thank you." They stared at each other. "Did you come for something?" Gopal asked, although he did not want to imply that he was trying to end the conversation.

"I wanted to borrow your lawn mower."

"Already?" April was just starting, and the dew did not evaporate until midday.

"Spring fever," she said.

Gopal's mind refused to provide a response to this. "Let me get you the mower."

They went to the garage. The warm sun on the back of his neck made Gopal hopeful. He believed that something would soon be said or done to delay Mrs. Shaw's departure, for certainly God could not leave him alone again. The garage smelled of must and gasoline. The lawn mower was in a shadowy corner with an aluminum ladder resting on it. "I haven't used it in a while," Gopal said, placing the ladder on the ground and smiling at Mrs. Shaw beside him. "But it should be fine." As he stood up, he suddenly felt aroused by Mrs. Shaw's large breasts, boy's haircut, and little-girl sneakers. Even her nostrils suggested a frank sexuality. Gopal wanted to put his hands on her waist and pull her toward him. And then he realized that he had.

"No. No," Mrs. Shaw said, laughing and putting her palms flat against his chest. "Not now." She pushed him away gently.

Gopal did not try kissing her again, but he was excited. Not now, he thought. He carefully poured gasoline into the lawn mower, wanting to appear calm, as if the two of them had already made some commitment and there was no need for nervousness. He pushed the lawn mower out onto the gravel driveway and jerked the cord to test the engine. Not now, not now, he thought, each time he tugged. He let the engine run for a minute. Mrs. Shaw stood silent beside him. Gopal felt like smiling, but wanted to make everything appear casual. "You can have it for as long as you need," he said.

"Thank you," Mrs. Shaw replied, and smiled. They looked at each other for a moment without saying anything. Then she rolled the lawn mower down the driveway and onto the road. She stopped, turned to look at him, and said, "I'll call."

"Good," Gopal answered, and watched her push the lawn mower down the road and up her driveway into the tin shack that huddled at its end. The driveway was separated from her ranch-style house by ten or fifteen feet of grass, and they were connected by a trampled path. Before she entered her house, Mrs. Shaw turned and looked at him as he stood at the top of his driveway. She smiled and waved.

When he went back into his house, Gopal was too excited to sleep. Before Mrs. Shaw, the only woman he had ever embraced was his wife, and a part of him assumed that it was now only a matter of time before he and Mrs. Shaw fell in love and his life resumed its normalcy. Oh, to live again as he had for nearly thirty years! Gopal thought, with such force that he shocked himself. Unable to sit, unable even to think coherently, he walked around his house.

HIS DAUGHTER'S DEPARTURE had made Gopal sick at heart for two or three weeks, but then she sank so completely from his thoughts that he questioned whether his pain had been hurt pride rather than grief. Gitu had been a graduate student and spent only a few weeks with them each year, so it was understandable that he would not miss her for long. But the swiftness with which the dense absence on the other side of his bed unknotted and evaporated made him wonder whether he had ever loved his wife. It made him think that his wife's abrupt decision never to return from her visit to India was as much his fault as God's. Anita, he thought, must have decided upon seeing Gitu leave that there was no more reason to stay, and that perhaps, after all, it was not too late to start again. Anita had gone to India at the end of November—a month after Gitu got on a Lufthansa flight to go live with her boyfriend in Germany—and a week later, over an echoing phone line, she told him of the guru and her enlightenment.

Perhaps if Gopal had not retired early from AT&T, he could have worked long hours and his wife's and daughter's slipping from his thoughts might have been mistaken for healing. But he had nothing to do. Most of his acquaintances had come by way of his wife, and when she left, Gopal did not call them, both because they had always been more Anita's friends than his and because he felt ashamed, as if his wife's departure revealed his inability to love her. At one point, around Christmas, he went to a dinner party, but he did not enjoy it. He found that he was not curious about other people's lives and did not want to talk about his own.

A month after Anita's departure a letter from her arrived—a blue aerogram, telling of the ashram, and of sweeping the courtyard, and of the daily prayers. Gopal responded immediately, but she never wrote again. His pride prevented him from trying to continue the correspondence, though he read her one letter so many times that he inadvertently memorized the Pune address. His brothers sent a flurry of long missives from India, on paper so thin that it was almost translucent, but his contact with them over the decades had been minimal, and the tragedy pushed them apart instead of pulling them closer.

Gitu sent a picture of herself wearing a yellow-and-blue ski jacket in the Swiss Alps. Gopal wrote her back in a stiff, formal way, and she responded with a breezy postcard to which he replied only after a long wait.

Other than this, Gopal had had little personal contact with the world. He was accustomed to getting up early and going to bed late, but now, since he had no work and no friends, after he spent the morning reading *The New York Times* and *The Home News & Tribune* front to back, Gopal felt adrift through the afternoon and evening. For a few weeks he tried to fill his days by showering and shaving twice daily, brushing his teeth after every snack and meal. But the purposelessness of this made him despair, and he stopped bathing altogether and instead began sleeping more and more, sometimes sixteen hours a day. He slept in the living room, long and narrow with high rectangular windows blocked by trees. At some point, in a burst of self-hate, Gopal moved his clothes from the bedroom closet to a corner of the living room, wanting to avoid comforting himself with any illusions that his life was normal.

But he yearned for his old life, the life of a clean kitchen, of a bedroom, of going out into the sun, and on a half-conscious level that morning Gopal decided to use the excitement of clasping Mrs. Shaw to change himself back to the man he had been. She might be spending time at his house, he thought, so he mopped the kitchen floor, moved back into his bedroom, vacuumed and dusted all the rooms. He spent most of the afternoon doing this, aware always of his humming lawn mower in the background. He had only to focus on it to make his heart race. Every now and then he would stop working and go to his bedroom window, where, from behind the curtains, he would stare at Mrs. Shaw. She had a red bandanna tied around her forehead, and he somehow found this appealing. That night he made himself an elaborate dinner with three dishes and a mango shake. For the first time in months Gopal watched the eleven o'clock news. He had the lights off and his feet up on a low table. Lebanon was being bombed again, and Gopal kept bursting into giggles for no reason. He tried to think of what he would do tomorrow. Gopal knew that he was happy and that to avoid depression he must keep himself busy until Mrs. Shaw called. He suddenly realized that he did not know Mrs. Shaw's first name. He padded into the darkened kitchen and looked at the phone diary. "Helen Shaw" was written in the big, loopy handwriting of his wife. Having his wife help him in this way did not bother him at all, and then he felt ashamed that it didn't.

THE NEXT DAY was Sunday, and Gopal anticipated it cheerfully, for the Sunday *Times* was frequently so thick that he could spend the whole day reading it. But this time he did not read it all the way through. He left the *Book Review* and the other features sections to fill time over the next few days. After eating a large breakfast—the idea of preparing elaborate meals had begun to appeal to him—he went for a haircut. Gopal had not left his house in several days. He rolled down the window of his blue Honda Civic and took the long way, past the lake, to the mall. Instead of going to his usual barber, he went to a hair stylist, where a woman with long nails and large, contented breasts shampooed his hair before cutting it. Then Gopal wandered around the mall, savoring its buttered-popcorn smell and enjoying the sight of the girls with their sometimes odd-colored hair. He went into some of the small shops and looked at clothes, and considered buying a half pound of cocoa amaretto coffee beans, although he had never cared much for coffee. After walking for nearly two hours, Gopal sat on a bench and ate an ice cream cone while reading an article in *Cosmopolitan* about what makes a good lover. He had seen the magazine in CVS and, noting the article mentioned on the cover, had been reminded how easily one can learn anything in America. Because Mrs. Shaw was an American, Gopal thought, he needed to do research into what might be expected of him. Although the article was about what makes a woman a good lover, it offered clues for men as well. Gopal felt confident that given time, Mrs. Shaw would love him. The article made attachment appear effortless. All you had to do was listen closely and speak honestly.

He returned home around five, and Mrs. Shaw called soon after. "If you want, you can come over now."

"All right," Gopal answered. He was calm. He showered and put on a blue cotton shirt and khaki slacks. When he stepped outside, the sky was turning pink and the air smelled of wet earth. He felt young, as if he had just arrived in America and the huge scale of things had made him a giant as well.

But when he rang Mrs. Shaw's doorbell, Gopal became nervous. He turned around and looked at the white clouds against the enormous sky. He heard footsteps and then the door swishing open and Mrs. Shaw's voice. "You look handsome," she said. Gopal faced her, smiling and uncomfortable. She wore a different sweatshirt, but still had on yesterday's jogging pants. She was barefoot. A yellow light shone behind her.

"Thank you," Gopal said, and then nervously added "Helen," to confirm their new relationship. "You look nice too." She did look pretty to him. Mrs. Shaw stepped aside to let him in. They were in a large room. In the center were two pale couches forming an L, with a television in front of them. Off to the side was a kitchenette—a stove, a refrigerator, and some cabinets over a sink and counter.

Seeing Gopal looking around, Mrs. Shaw said, "There are two bedrooms in the back, and a bathroom. Would you like anything to drink? I have juice, if you want." She walked to the kitchen.

"What are you going to have?" Gopal asked, following her. "If you have something, I'll have something." Then he felt embarrassed. Mrs. Shaw had not dressed up; obviously, "Not now" had been a polite rebuff.

"I was going to have a gin and tonic," she said, opening the refrigerator and standing before it with one hand on her hip.

"I would like that too." Gopal came close to her and with a dart kissed her on the lips. She did not resist, but neither did she respond. Her lips were chapped. Gopal pulled away and let her make the drinks. He had hoped the kiss would tell him something of what to expect.

They sat side by side on a couch and sipped their drinks. A table lamp cast a diffused light over them.

"Thank you for letting me borrow the lawn mower."

"It's nothing." There was a long pause. Gopal could not think of anything to say. *Cosmopolitan* had suggested trying to learn as much as possible about your lover, so he asked, "What's your favorite color?"

"Why?"

"I want to know everything about you."

"That's sweet," Mrs. Shaw said, and patted his hand. Gopal felt embarrassed and looked down. He did not know whether he should have spoken so frankly, but part of his intention had been to flatter her with his interest. "I don't have one," she said. She kept her hand on his.

Gopal suddenly thought that they might make love tonight, and he felt his heart kick. "Tell me all about yourself," he said with a voice full of feeling. "Where were you born?"

"I was born in Jersey City on May fifth, but I won't tell you the year." Gopal tried to grin gamely and memorize the date. A part of him was disturbed that she did not feel comfortable enough with him to reveal her age.

"Did you grow up there?" he asked, taking a sip of the gin and tonic. Gopal drank slowly, because he knew that he could not hold his alcohol. He saw that Mrs. Shaw's toes were painted bright red. Anita had never used nail polish, and Gopal wondered what a woman who would paint her toenails might do.

"I moved to Newark when I was three. My parents ran a newspaper-and-candy shop. We sold greeting cards, stamps." Mrs. Shaw had nearly finished her drink. "They opened at eight in the morning and closed at seven thirty at night. Six days a week." When she paused between swallows, she rested the glass on her knee.

Gopal had never known anyone who worked in such a shop, and he became genuinely interested in what she was saying. He remembered his lack of interest at the Christmas party and wondered whether it was the possibility of sex that made him fascinated with Mrs. Shaw's story. "Were you a happy child?" he asked, grinning broadly and then bringing the grin to a quick end, because he did not want to appear ironic. The half glass that Gopal had drunk had already begun to make him feel light-headed and gay.

"Oh, pretty happy," she said, "although I liked to think of myself as serious. I would look at the evening sky and think that no one else had felt what I was feeling." Mrs. Shaw's understanding of her own feelings disconcerted Gopal and made him momentarily think that he wasn't learning anything important, or that she was in some way independent of her past and thus incapable of the sentimental attachments through which he expected her love for him to grow.

Cosmopolitan had recommended that both partners reveal themselves, so Gopal decided to tell a story about himself. He did not believe that being honest about himself would actually change him. Rather, he thought the deliberateness of telling the story would rob it of the power to make him vulnerable. He started to say something, but the words twisted in his mouth, and he said, "You know, I don't really drink much." Gopal felt embarrassed by the non sequitur. He thought he sounded foolish, though he had hoped that the story he would tell would make him appear sensitive.

"I kind of guessed that from the juices," she said, smiling. Gopal laughed.

He tried to say what he had wanted to confess earlier. "I associate drinking with being American, and I haven't been able to truly Americanize. On my daughter's nineteenth birthday we took her to dinner and a movie, but we didn't talk much, and the dinner finished earlier than we had expected it would. The restaurant was in a mall, and we had nothing to do until the movie started, so we wandered around Foodtown." Gopal thought he sounded pathetic, so he tried to shift the story. "After all my years in America, I am still astonished by those huge grocery stores and enjoy walking in them. But my daughter is an American, so our wandering around in Foodtown must have been very strange for her. She doesn't know Hindi, and her parents must seem very strange." Gopal noticed that his heart was racing. He wondered if he was sadder than he knew.

"That's sweet," Mrs. Shaw said. The brevity of her response made Gopal nervous.

Mrs. Shaw kissed his cheek. Her lips were dry, Gopal noticed. He turned slightly so that their lips could touch. They kissed again. Mrs. Shaw opened her lips and closed her eyes. They kissed for a long time. When they pulled apart, they continued their conversation calmly, as if they were accustomed to each other. "I didn't go into a big grocery store until I was in college," she said. "We always went to the small shops around us. When I first saw those long aisles, I wondered what happens to the food if no one buys it. I was living then with a man who was seven or eight years older than I, and when I told him, he laughed at me, and I felt so young." She stopped and then added, "I ended up leaving him because he always made me feel young." Her face was only an inch or two from Gopal's. "Now I'd marry someone who could make me feel that way." Gopal felt his romantic feelings drain away at the idea of how many men she had slept with. But the fact that Mrs. Shaw and he had experienced something similar removed some of the loneliness he was feeling, and Mrs. Shaw had large breasts. They began kissing again. Soon they were tussling and groping on the floor.

Her bed was large and low to the ground. Behind it was a window, and although the shade was drawn, the lights of passing cars cast patterns on the opposing wall. Gopal lay next to Mrs. Shaw and watched the shadows change. He felt his head and found that his hair was standing up on either side like horns. The shock of seeing a new naked body, so different in its amplitude from his wife's, had been exciting. A part of him was giddy with this, as if he had checked his bank balance and discovered that he had thousands more than he expected. "You are very beautiful," he said, for *Cosmopolitan* had advised saying this after making love. Mrs. Shaw rolled over and kissed his shoulder.

"No I'm not. I'm kind of fat, and my nose is strange. But thank you," she said. Gopal looked at her and saw that even when her mouth was slack, the lines around it were deep. "You look like you've been rolled around in a dryer," she said, and laughed. Her laughter was sudden and confident. He had not noticed it before, and it made him laugh as well.

They became silent and lay quietly for several minutes, and when Gopal began feeling self-conscious, he said, "Describe the first house you lived in."

Mrs. Shaw sat up. Her stomach bulged, and her breasts drooped. She saw him looking and pulled her knees to her chest. "You're very thoughtful," she said.

Gopal felt flattered. "Oh, it's not thoughtfulness."

"I guess if it weren't for your accent, the questions would sound artificial," she said. Gopal felt his stomach clench. "I lived in a block of small houses that the Army built for returning GIs. They were all drab, and the lawns ran into each other. They were near Newark airport. I liked to sit at my window and watch the planes land."

"Your house was two stories?"

"Yes. And my room was on the second floor. Tell me about yourself."

"I am the third of five brothers. We grew up in a small, poor village. I got my first pair of shoes when I left high school." As Gopal was telling her the story, he remembered how he used to make Gitu feel lazy with stories of his childhood, and his voice fell. "Everybody was like us, so I never thought of myself as poor."

They talked this way for half an hour, with Gopal asking most of the questions and trying to discover where Mrs. Shaw was vulnerable and how this vulnerability made him attractive to her. Although she answered his questions candidly, Gopal could not find the unhappy childhood or the trauma of an abandoned wife that might explain the urgency of this moment in bed. "I was planning to leave my husband," she explained casually. "He was crazy. Almost literally. He thought he was going to be a senator or a captain of industry. He wasn't registered to vote. He knew nothing about business. Once, he invested almost everything we had in a hydroponic farm in Southampton. With him I was always scared of being poor. He used to spend two hundred dollars a week on lottery tickets, and he would save the old tickets in shoe boxes in the garage." Gopal did not personally know any Indian who was divorced, and he had never been intimate enough with an American to learn what a divorce was like, but he had expected something more painful—tears and recriminations. The details she gave made the story sound practiced, and he began to think that he would never have a hold over Mrs. Shaw.

Around eight Mrs. Shaw said, "I am going to do my bills tonight." Gopal had been wondering whether she wanted him to have dinner with her and spend the night. He would have liked to, but he did not protest.

As she closed the door behind him, Mrs. Shaw said, "The lawn mower's in the back. If you want it." Night had come, and the stars were out. As Gopal pushed the lawn mower down the road, he wished that he loved Mrs. Shaw and that she loved him.

He had left the kitchen light on by mistake, and its glow was comforting. "Come, come, cheer up," he said aloud, pacing in the kitchen. "You have a lover." He tried to smile and grimaced instead. "You can make love as often as you want. Be happy." He started preparing dinner. He fried okra and steam-cooked lentils. He made both rice and bread.

As he ate, Gopal watched a television movie about a woman who had been in a coma for twenty years and suddenly woke up one day; adding to her confusion, she was pregnant. After washing the dishes he finished the article in *Cosmopolitan* that he had begun reading in the mall. The article was the second of two parts, and it mentioned that when leaving after making love for the first time, one should always arrange the next meeting. Gopal had not done this, and he phoned Mrs. Shaw.

He used the phone in the kitchen, and as he waited for her to pick up, he wondered whether he should introduce himself or assume that she would recognize his voice. "Hi, Helen," he blurted out as soon as she said "Hello." "I was just thinking of you and thought I'd call." He felt more nervous now than he had while he was with her.

"That's sweet," she said, with what Gopal thought was tenderness. "How are you?"

"I just had dinner. Did you eat?" He imagined her sitting on the floor between the couches with a pile of receipts before her. She would have a small pencil in her hand.

"I'm not hungry. I normally make myself an omelet for dinner, but I didn't want to tonight. I'm having another drink." Then, self-conscious, she added, "Otherwise I grind my teeth. I started after my divorce and I didn't have health insurance or enough money to go to a dentist." Gopal wanted to ask if she still ground her teeth, but he did not want to imply anything.

"Would you like to have dinner tomorrow? I'll cook." They agreed to meet at six. The conversation continued for a few minutes longer, and when Gopal hung up, he was pleased at how well he had handled things.

While lying in bed, waiting for sleep, Gopal read another article in *Cosmopolitan*, about job pressure's effects on one's sex life. He had enjoyed both articles and was happy with himself for his efforts at understanding Mrs. Shaw. He fell asleep smiling.

THE NEXT DAY, after reading the papers, Gopal went to the library to read the first part of the *Cosmopolitan* article. He ended up reading articles from *Elle, Redbook, Glamour, Mademoiselle,* and *Family Circle,* and one from *Reader's Digest* "How to Tell If Your Marriage Is on the Rocks." He tried to memorize jokes from the "Laughter Is the Best Medicine" section, so that he would never be at a loss for conversation.

Gopal arrived at home by four and began cooking. Dinner was pleasant, though they ate in the kitchen, which was lit with buzzing fluorescent tubes. Gopal worried that yesterday's love-making might have been a fluke. Soon after they finished the meal, however, they were on the couch, struggling with each other's clothing.

Gopal wanted Mrs. Shaw to spend the night, but she refused, saying that she had not slept a full night with anyone since her divorce. At first Gopal was touched by this. They lay on his bed in the dark. The alarm clock on the lampstand said 9:12 in big red figures. "Why?" Gopal asked, rolling over and resting his cheek on her cool shoulder. He wanted to reassure her that he was eager to listen.

"I think I'm a serial monogamist and I don't want to make things too complicated." She twisted a lock of his hair around her middle finger. "It isn't because of you, sweetie. It's with every man."

"Oh," Gopal said, hurt by the idea of other men and disillusioned about her motives. He continued believing, however, that now that they were lovers, the power of his concern would make her love him back. One of the articles he had read that day had suggested that people become dependent in spite of themselves when they are constantly cared for. So he made himself relax and act understanding.

Gopal went to bed an hour after Mrs. Shaw left. Before going to sleep he called her and wished her good night. He began calling her frequently after that, two or three times a day. Over the next few weeks Gopal found himself becoming coy and playful with her. When Mrs. Shaw picked up the phone, he made panting noises, and she laughed at him. She liked his being childlike with her. Sometimes she would point to a spot on his chest, and he would look down, even though he knew nothing was there, so that she could tap his nose. When they made love, she was thoughtful about asking what pleased him, and Gopal learned from this and began asking her the same. They saw each other nearly every day, though sometimes only briefly, for a few minutes in the evening or at night. But Gopal continued to feel nervous around her, as if he were somehow imposing. If she phoned him and invited him over, he was always flattered. As Gopal learned more about Mrs. Shaw, he began thinking she was very smart. She read constantly, primarily history and economics. He was always surprised, therefore, when she became moody and sentimental and talked about how loneliness is incurable. Gopal liked Mrs. Shaw in this mood, because it made him feel needed, but he felt ashamed that he was so insecure. When she did not laugh at a joke, Gopal doubted that she would ever love him. When they were in bed together and he thought she might be looking at him, he kept his stomach sucked in.

THIS SENSE OF PRECARIOUSNESS made Gopal try developing other supports for himself. One morning early in his involvement with Mrs. Shaw he phoned an Indian engineer with whom he had worked on a project about corrosion of copper wires and who had also taken early retirement from AT&T. They had met briefly several times since then and had agreed each time to get together again, but neither had made the effort. Gopal waited until eleven before calling, because he felt that any earlier would make him sound needy. A woman picked up the phone. She told him to wait a minute as she called for Rishi. Gopal felt vaguely deceitful, as if he were trying to pass himself off as just like everyone else, although his wife and child had left him.

"I haven't been doing much," he confessed immediately to Rishi. "I read a lot." When Rishi asked what, Gopal answered "Magazines," with embarrassment. They were silent then.

Gopal did not want to ask Rishi immediately if he would like to meet for dinner, so he hunted desperately for a conversational opening. He was sitting in the kitchen. He looked at the sunlight on the newspaper before him and remembered that he could ask Rishi questions. "How are you doing?"

"It isn't like India," Rishi responded. "In India the older you are, the closer you are to the center of attention. Here you have to keep going. Your children are away and you have nothing to do. I would go back, but Ratha doesn't want to. America is much better for women."

Gopal felt a rush of relief that Rishi had spoken so much. "Are you just at home or are you doing something part-time?"

"I am the president of the Indian Cultural Association," Rishi said boastfully.

"That's wonderful," Gopal said, and with a leap added, "I want to get involved in that more, now that I have time."

"We always need help. We are going to have a fair," Rishi said. "It's on the twenty-fourth, next month. We need help coordinating things, arranging food, putting up flyers."

"I can help," Gopal said. They decided that he should come to Rishi's house on Wednesday, two days later.

Gopal was about to hang up when Rishi added, "I heard about your family." Gopal felt as if he had been caught in a lie. "I am sorry," Rishi said.

Gopal was quiet for a moment and then said, "Thank you." He did not know whether he should pretend to be sad. "It takes some getting used to," he said, "but you can go on from nearly anything."

Gopal went to see Rishi that Wednesday, and on Sunday he attended a board meeting to plan for the fair. He told jokes about a nearsighted snake and a water hose, and about a golf instructor and God. One of the men he met there invited him to dinner.

Mrs. Shaw, however, continued to dominate his thoughts. The more they made love, the more absorbed Gopal became in the texture of her nipples in his mouth and the heft of her hips in his hands. He thought of this in the shower, while driving, while stirring his cereal. Two or three times over the next month Gopal picked her up during her lunch hour and they hurried home to make love. They would make love and then talk. Mrs. Shaw had once worked at a dry cleaner, and Gopal found this fascinating. He had met only one person in his life before Mrs. Shaw who had worked in a dry-cleaning business, and that was different, because it was in India, where dry cleaning still had the glamour of advancing technology. Being the lover of someone who had worked in a dry-cleaning business made Gopal feel strange. It made him think that the world was huge beyond comprehension, and to spend his time trying to control his own small world was inefficient. Gopal began thinking that he loved Mrs. Shaw. He started listening to the golden oldies station in the car, so that he could hear what she had heard in her youth.

Mrs. Shaw would ask about his life, and Gopal tried to tell her everything she wanted to know in as much detail as possible. Once, he told her of how he had begun worrying when his daughter was finishing high school that she was going to slip from his life. To show that he loved her, he had arbitrarily forbidden her to ski, claiming that skiing was dangerous. He had hoped that she would find this quaintly immigrant, but she was just angry. At first the words twisted in his mouth, and he spoke to Mrs. Shaw about skiing in general. Only with an effort could he tell her about his fight with Gitu. Mrs. Shaw did not say anything at first. Then she said, "It's all right if you were that way once, as long as you aren't that way now." Listening to her, Gopal suddenly felt angry.

"Why do you talk like this?" he asked.

"What?"

"When you talk about how your breasts fall or how your behind is too wide, I always say that's not true. I always see you with eyes that make you beautiful."

"Because I want the truth," she said, also angry.

Gopal became quiet. Her desire for honesty appeared to refute all his delicate and constant manipulations. Was he actually in love with her, he wondered, or was this love just a way to avoid loneliness? And did it matter that so much of what he did was conscious?

He questioned his love more and more as the day of the Indian festival approached, and Gopal realized that he was delaying asking Mrs. Shaw to come with him. She knew about the fair but had not mentioned her feelings. Gopal told himself that she would feel uncomfortable among so many Indians, but he knew that he hadn't asked her because bringing her would make him feel awkward. For some reason he was nervous that word of Mrs. Shaw might get to his wife and daughter. He was also anxious about what the Indians with whom he had recently become friendly would think. He had met mixed couples at Indian parties before, and they were always treated with the deference usually reserved for cripples. If Mrs. Shaw had been of any sort of marginalized ethnic group—a first-generation immigrant, for instance—then things might have been easier.

The festival was held in the Edison First Aid Squad's square blue-and-white building. A children's dance troupe performed in red dresses so stiff with gold thread that the girls appeared to hobble as they moved about the center of the concrete floor. A balding comedian in oxblood shoes and a white suit performed. Light folding tables along one wall were precariously laden with large pots, pans, and trays of food. Gopal stood in a corner with several men who had retired from AT&T and, slightly drunk, he improvised on jokes he had read in *1,001 Polish Jokes.* The Poles became Sikhs, but the rest remained the same. He was laughing and feeling proud that he could so easily become the center of attention, but he felt lonely at the thought that when the food was served, the men at his side would drift away to join their families and he would be alone. After listening to talk of someone's marriage, he began thinking about Mrs. Shaw. The men were clustered together, and the women conversed separately. They will go home and make love and not talk, Gopal thought. Then he felt sad and frightened. To make amends for his guilt at not bringing Mrs. Shaw along, he told a bearded man with yellow teeth, "These Sikhs aren't so bad. They are the smartest ones in India, and no one can match a Sikh for courage." Then Gopal felt dazed and ready to leave.

WHEN GOPAL PULLED into his driveway, it was late afternoon. His head felt oddly still, as it always did when alcohol started wearing off, but Gopal knew that he was drunk enough to do something foolish. He parked and walked down the road to Mrs. Shaw's. He wondered if she would be in. Pale tulips bloomed in a thin, uneven row in front of her house. The sight of them made him hopeful.

Mrs. Shaw opened the door before he could knock. For a moment Gopal did not say anything. She was wearing a denim skirt and a sleeveless white shirt. She smiled at him. Gopal spoke solemnly and from far off. "I love you," he said to her for the first time. "I am sorry I didn't invite you to the fair." He waited a moment for his statement to sink in and for her to respond with a similar endearment. When she did not, he repeated, "I love you."

Then she said, "Thank you," and told him not to worry about the fair. She invited him in. Gopal was confused and flustered by her reticence. He began feeling awkward about his confession. They kissed briefly, and then Gopal went home.

The next night, as they sat together watching TV in his living room, Mrs. Shaw suddenly turned to Gopal and said, "You really do love me, don't you?" Although Gopal had expected the question, he was momentarily disconcerted by it, because it made him wonder what love was and whether he was capable of it. But he did not think that this was the time to quibble over semantics. After being silent long enough to suggest that he was struggling with his vulnerability, Gopal said yes and waited for Mrs. Shaw's response. Again she did not confess her love. She kissed his forehead tenderly. This show of sentiment made Gopal angry, but he said nothing. He was glad, though, when Mrs. Shaw left that night.

The next day Gopal waited for Mrs. Shaw to return home from work. He had decided that the time had come for the next step in their relationship. As soon as he saw her struggle through her doorway, hugging sacks of groceries, Gopal phoned. He stood on the steps to his house, with the extension cord trailing over one shoulder, and looked at her house and at her rusted and exhausted-looking station wagon, which he had begun to associate strongly and warmly with the broad sweep of Mrs. Shaw's life. Gopal nearly said "I missed you" when she picked up the phone, but he became embarrassed and asked, "How was your day?"

"Fine," she said, and Gopal imagined her moving about the kitchen, putting away whatever she had bought, placing the teakettle on the stove, and sorting her mail on the kitchen table. This image of domesticity and independence moved him deeply. "There's a guidance counselor who is dying of cancer," she said, "and his friends are having a party for him, and they put up a sign saying 'RSVP with your money now! Henry can't wait for the party!' " Gopal and Mrs. Shaw laughed.

"Let's do something," he said.

"What?"

Gopal had not thought this part out. He wanted to do something romantic that would last until bedtime, so that he could pressure her to spend the night. "Would you like to have dinner?"

"Sure," she said. Gopal was pleased. He had gone to a liquor store a few days earlier and bought wine, just in case he had an opportunity to get Mrs. Shaw drunk and get her to fall asleep beside him.

Gopal plied Mrs. Shaw with wine as they ate the linguine he had cooked. They sat in the kitchen, but he had turned off the fluorescent lights and lit a candle. By the third glass Gopal was feeling very brave; he placed his hand on her inner thigh.

"My mother and father," Mrs. Shaw said halfway through the meal, pointing at him with her fork and speaking with the deliberateness of the drunk, "convinced me that people are not meant to live together for long periods of time." She was speaking in response to Gopal's hint earlier that only over time and through living together could people get to know each other properly. "If you know someone that well, you are bound to be disappointed."

"Maybe that's because you haven't met the right person," Gopal answered, feeling awkward for saying something that could be considered arrogant when he was trying to appear vulnerable.

"I don't think there is a right person. Not for me. To fall in love I think you need a certain suspension of disbelief, which I don't think I am capable of."

Gopal wondered whether Mrs. Shaw believed what she was

saying or was trying not to hurt his feelings by revealing that she couldn't love him. He stopped eating.

Mrs. Shaw stared at him. She put her fork down and said, "I love you. I love how you care for me and how gentle you are."

Gopal smiled. Perhaps, he thought, the first part of her statement had been a preface to a confession that he mattered so much that she was willing to make an exception for him. "I love you too," Gopal said. "I love how funny and smart and honest you are. You are very beautiful." He leaned over slightly to suggest that he wanted to kiss her, but Mrs. Shaw did not respond.

Her face was stiff. "I love you," she said again, and Gopal became nervous. "But I am not in love with you." She stopped and stared at Gopal.

Gopal felt confused. "What's the difference?"

"When you are in love, you never think about yourself, because you love the other person so completely. I've lived too long to think anyone is that perfect." Gopal still didn't understand the distinction, but he was too embarrassed to ask more. It was only fair, a part of him thought, that God would punish him this way for driving away his wife and child. How could anyone love him?

Mrs. Shaw took his hands in hers. "I think we should take a little break from each other, so we don't get confused. Being with you, I'm getting confused too. We should see other people."

"Oh." Gopal's chest hurt despite his understanding of the justice of what was happening.

"I don't want to hide anything. I love you. I truly love you. You are the kindest lover I've ever had."

"Oh."

For a week after this Gopal observed that Mrs. Shaw did not bring another man to her house. He went to the Sunday board meeting of the cultural association, where he regaled the members with jokes from *Reader's Digest*. He taught his first Hindi class to children at the temple. He took his car to be serviced. Gopal did all these things. He ate. He slept. He even made love to Mrs. Shaw once, and until she asked him to leave, he thought everything was all right again.

Then, one night, Gopal was awakened at a little after three by a car pulling out of Mrs. Shaw's driveway. It is just a friend, he thought, standing by his bedroom window and watching the Toyota move down the road. Gopal tried falling asleep again, but he could not, though he was not thinking of anything in particular. His mind was blank, but sleep did not come.

I will not call her, Gopal thought in the morning. And as he was dialing her, he thought he would hang up before all the numbers had been pressed. He heard the receiver being lifted on the other side and Mrs. Shaw saying "Hello." He did not say anything. "Don't do this, Gopal," she said softly. "Don't hurt me."

"Hi," Gopal whispered, wanting very much to hurt her. He leaned his head against the kitchen wall. His face twitched as he whispered, "I'm sorry."

"Don't be that way. I love you. I didn't want to hurt you. That's why I told you."

"I know."

"All right?"

"Yes." They were silent for a long time. Then Gopal hung up. He wondered if she would call back.

⁂

FOR THE NEXT FEW WEEKS Gopal tried to spend as little time as possible in his house. He read the morning papers in the library, and then had lunch at a diner, and then went back to the library. On Sundays he spent all day at the mall. His anger at Mrs. Shaw soon disappeared, because he thought that the blame for her leaving lay with him. Gopal continued, however, to avoid home, because he did not want to experience the jealousy that would keep him awake all night. Only if he arrived late enough and tired enough could he fall asleep. In the evening Gopal either went to the temple and helped at the seven o'clock service or visited one of his new acquaintances. But over the weeks he exhausted the kindheartedness of his acquaintances and had a disagreement with one man's wife, and he was forced to return home.

The first few evenings he spent at home Gopal thought he would have to flee his house in despair. He slept awkwardly, waking at the barest rustle outside his window, thinking that a car was pulling out of Mrs. Shaw's driveway. The days were easier than the nights, especially when Mrs. Shaw was away at work. Gopal would sleep a few hours at night and then nap during the day, but this left him exhausted and dizzy. In the afternoon he liked to sit on the steps and read the paper, pausing occasionally to look at her house. He liked the sun sliding up its walls. Sometimes he was sitting outside when she drove home from work. Mrs. Shaw waved to him once or twice, but he did not respond, not because he was angry but because he felt himself become so still at the sight of her that he could neither wave nor smile.

A month and a half after they separated, Gopal still could not sleep at night if he thought there were two cars in Mrs. Shaw's driveway. Once, after a series of sleepless nights, he was up until three watching a dark shape behind Mrs. Shaw's station wagon. He waited by his bedroom window, paralyzed with fear and hope, for a car to pass in front of her house and strike the shape with its headlights. After a long time in which no car went by, Gopal decided to check for himself.

He started across his lawn crouched over and running. The air was warm and smelled of jasmine, and Gopal was so tired he thought he might spill to the ground. After a few steps he stopped and straightened up. The sky was clear, and there were so many stars that Gopal felt as if he were in his village in India. The houses along the street were dark and drawn in on themselves. Even in India, he thought, late at night the houses look like sleeping faces. He remembered how surprised he had been by the pitched roofs of American houses when he had first come here, and how this had made him yearn to return to India, where he could sleep on the roof. He started across the lawn again. Gopal walked slowly, and he felt as if he were crossing a great distance.

The station wagon stood battered and alone, smelling faintly of gasoline and the day's heat. Gopal leaned against its hood. The station wagon was so old that the odometer had gone all the way around. Like me, he thought, and like Helen, too. This is who we are, he thought—dusty, corroded, and dented from our voyages, with our unflagging hearts rattling on inside. We are made who we are by the dust and corrosion and dents and unflagging hearts. Why should we need anything else to fall in love? he wondered. We learn and change and get better. He leaned against the car for a minute or two. Fireflies swung flickering in the breeze. Then he walked home.

Gopal woke early and showered and shaved and made breakfast. He brushed his teeth after eating and felt his cheeks to see whether he should shave again, this time against the grain. At nine he crossed his lawn and rang Mrs. Shaw's doorbell. He had to ring it several times before he heard her footsteps. When she opened the door and saw him, Mrs. Shaw drew back as if she were afraid. Gopal felt sad that she could think he might hurt her. "May I come in?" he asked. She stared at him. He saw mascara stains beneath her eyes and silver strands mingled with her red hair. He thought he had never seen a woman as beautiful or as gallant.

SURROUNDED BY SLEEP

One August afternoon, when Ajay was ten years old, his elder brother, Birju, dove into a pool and struck his head on the cement bottom. For three minutes, he lay there unconscious. Two boys continued to swim, kicking and splashing, until finally Birju was spotted below them. Water had entered through his nose and mouth. It had filled his stomach. His lungs had collapsed. By the time he was pulled out, he could no longer think, talk, chew, or roll over in his sleep.

Ajay's family had moved from India to Queens, New York, two years earlier. The accident occurred during the boys' summer vacation, on a visit with their aunt and uncle in Arlington, Virginia. After the accident, Ajay's mother came to Arlington, where she waited to see if Birju would recover. At the hospital, she told the doctors and nurses that her son had been accepted into the Bronx High School of Science, in the hope that by highlighting his intelligence she would move them to make a greater effort on his behalf. Within a few weeks of the accident, the insurance company said that Birju should be transferred to a less expensive care facility, a long-term one. But only a few of these were any good, and those were full, and Ajay's mother refused to move Birju until a space opened in one of them. So she remained in Arlington, and Ajay stayed, too, and his father visited from Queens on the weekends when he wasn't working. Ajay was enrolled at the local public school and in September he started fifth grade.

Before the accident, Ajay had never prayed much. In India, he and his brother used to go with their mother to the temple every Tuesday night, but that was mostly because there was a good dosa restaurant nearby. In America, his family went to a temple only on important holy days and birthdays. But shortly after Ajay's mother came to Arlington, she moved into the room that he and his brother had shared during the summer and made an altar in a corner. She threw an old flowered sheet over a cardboard box that had once held a television. On top, she put a clay lamp, an incense-stick holder, and postcards depicting various gods. There was also a postcard of Mahatma Gandhi. She explained to Ajay that God could take any form; the picture of Mahatma Gandhi was there because he had appeared to her in a dream after the accident and told her that Birju would recover and become a surgeon. Now she and Ajay prayed for at least half an hour before the altar every morning and night.

At first, she prayed with absolute humility. "Whatever you do will be good because you are doing it," she murmured to post-cards of Ram and Shivaji, daubing their lips with water and rice. Mahatma Gandhi got only water, because he did not like to eat. As weeks passed and Birju did not recover in time to go to the Bronx High School of Science for the first day of classes, his mother began doing things that called attention to her piety. She sometimes held the prayer lamp until it blistered her palms. Instead of kneeling before the altar, she lay facedown. She fasted twice a week. Her attempts to sway God were not so different from Ajay's performing somersaults to amuse his aunt, and they made God seem human to Ajay.

One morning, as Ajay knelt before the altar, he traced an Om, a cross, and a Star of David into the pile of the carpet. Beneath these, he traced an *S*, for Superman, inside an upside-down triangle. His mother came up beside him.

"What are you praying for?" she asked. She had her hat on, a thick gray knitted one that a man might wear. The tracings went against the weave of the carpet and were darker than the surrounding nap. Pretending to examine them, Ajay leaned forward and put his hand over the *S*. His mother did not mind the Christian and Jewish symbols—they were for commonly recognized gods, after all—but she could not tolerate his praying to Superman. She'd caught him doing so once, several weeks earlier, and had become very angry, as if Ajay's faith in Superman made her faith in Ram ridiculous. "Right in front of God," she had said several times.

Ajay, in his nervousness, spoke the truth. "I'm asking God to give me a hundred percent on the math test."

His mother was silent for a moment.

"What if God says you can have the math grade but then Birju will have to be sick a little while longer?" she asked.

Ajay kept quiet. He could hear cars on the road outside. He knew that his mother wanted to bewail her misfortune before God so that God would feel guilty. He looked at the postcard of Mahatma Gandhi. It was a black-and-white photo of him walking down a city street with an enormous crowd trailing behind him. Ajay thought of how, before the accident, Birju had been so modest that he would not leave the bathroom until he was fully dressed. Now he had rashes on his penis from the catheter that carried his urine into a translucent bag hanging from the guardrail of his bed.

His mother asked again, "Would you say, 'Let him be sick a little while longer'?"

"Are you going to tell me the story about Uncle Naveen again?" he asked.

"Why shouldn't I? When I was sick, as a girl, your uncle walked seven times around the temple and asked God to let him fail his exams just as long as I got better."

"If I failed the math test and told you that story, you'd slap me and ask what one has to do with the other."

His mother turned to the altar.

"What sort of sons did you give me, God?" she asked. "One you drown, the other is this selfish fool."

"I will fast today so that God puts some sense in me," Ajay said, glancing away from the altar and up at his mother. He liked the drama of fasting.

"No, you are a growing boy." His mother knelt down beside him and said to the altar, "He is stupid, but he has a good heart."

PRAYER, AJAY THOUGHT, should appeal with humility and an open heart to some greater force. But the praying that he and his mother did felt sly and confused. By treating God as someone to bargain with, it seemed to him they prayed as if they were casting a spell.

This meant that it was possible to do away with the presence of God entirely. For example, Ajay's mother had recently asked a relative in India to drive a nail into a holy tree and tie a saffron thread to the nail on Birju's behalf. Ajay invented his own ritual. On his way to school each morning, he passed a thick tree rooted half on the sidewalk and half on the road. One day, Ajay got the idea that if he circled the tree seven times, touching the north side every other time, he would have a lucky day. From then on, he did it every morning, although he felt embarrassed and always looked around beforehand to make sure no one was watching.

One night, Ajay asked God whether he minded being prayed to only in need.

"You think of your toe only when you stub it," God replied. God looked like Clark Kent. He wore a gray cardigan, slacks, and thick glasses, and had a forelock that curled just as Ajay's did.

God and Ajay had begun talking occasionally after Birju drowned. Now they talked most nights while Ajay lay in bed and waited for sleep. God sat at the foot of Ajay's mattress. His mother's mattress lay parallel to his, a few feet away. Originally, God had appeared to Ajay as Krishna, but Ajay had felt foolish discussing brain damage with a blue God who held a flute and wore a dhoti.

"You're not angry with me for touching the tree and all that?"

"No. I'm flexible."

"I respect you. The tree is just a way of praying to you," Ajay assured God.

God laughed. "I am not too caught up in formalities."

Ajay was quiet. He was convinced that he had been marked as special by Birju's accident. The beginnings of all heroes are distinguished by misfortune. Superman and Batman were both orphans. Krishna was separated from his parents at birth. The god Ram had to spend fourteen years in a forest. Ajay waited to speak until it would not appear improper to begin talking about himself.

"How famous will I be?" he asked, finally.

"I can't tell you the future," God answered.

Ajay asked, "Why not?"

"Even if I told you something, later I might change my mind."

"But it might be harder to change your mind after you have said something will happen."

God laughed again. "You'll be so famous that fame will be a problem."

Ajay sighed. His mother snorted and rolled over.

"I want Birju's drowning to lead to something," he said to God.

"He won't be forgotten."

"I can't just be famous, though. I need to be rich too, to take care of Mummy and Daddy and pay for Birju's hospital bills."

"You are always practical." God had a soulful and pitying voice and God's sympathy made Ajay imagine himself as a truly tragic figure, like Amitabh Bachchan in the movie *Trishul*.

"I have responsibilities," Ajay said. He was so excited at the thought of his possible greatness that he knew he would have difficulty sleeping. Perhaps he would have to go read in the bathroom.

"You can hardly imagine the life ahead," God said.

Even though God's tone promised greatness, the idea of the future frightened Ajay. He opened his eyes. There was light coming from the street. The room was cold and had a smell of must and incense. His aunt and uncle's house was a narrow two-story home next to a four-lane road. The apartment building with the pool where Birju had drowned was a few blocks up the road, one in a cluster of tall brick buildings with stucco fronts. Ajay pulled the blanket tighter around him. In India, he could not have imagined the reality of his life in America: the thick smell of meat in the school cafeteria, the many television channels. And, of course, he could not have imagined Birju's accident, or the hospital where he spent so much time.

⁂

THE HOSPITAL WAS BORING. Vinod, Ajay's cousin, picked him up after school and dropped him off there almost every day. Vinod was twenty-two. In addition to attending county college and studying computer programming, he worked at a 7-Eleven near Ajay's school. He often brought Ajay hot chocolate and a comic from the store, which had to be returned, so Ajay was not allowed to open it until he had wiped his hands.

Vinod usually asked him a riddle on the way to the hospital. "Why are manhole covers round?" It took Ajay half the ride to admit that he did not know. He was having difficulty talking. He didn't know why. The only time he could talk easily was when he was with God. The explanation he gave himself for this was that, just as he couldn't chew when there was too much in his mouth, he couldn't talk when there were too many thoughts in his head.

When Ajay got to Birju's room, he greeted him as if he were all right. "Hello, lazy. How much longer are you going to sleep?" His mother was always there. She got up and hugged Ajay. She asked how school had been, and he didn't know what to say. In music class, the teacher sang a song about a sailor who had bared his breast before jumping into the sea. This had caused the other students to giggle. But Ajay could not say the word "breast" to his mother without blushing. He had also cried. He'd been thinking of how Birju's accident had made his own life mysterious and confused. What would happen next? Would Birju die or would he go on as he was? Where would they live? Usually when Ajay cried in school, he was told to go outside. But it had been raining, and the teacher had sent him into the hallway. He sat on the floor and wept. Any mention of this would upset his mother. And so he said nothing had happened that day.

Sometimes when Ajay arrived his mother was on the phone, telling his father that she missed him and was expecting to see him on Friday. His father took a Greyhound bus most Fridays from Queens to Arlington, returning on Sunday night in time to work the next day. He was a bookkeeper for a department store. Before the accident, Ajay had thought of his parents as the same person: MummyDaddy. Now, when he saw his father praying stiffly or when his father failed to say hello to Birju in his hospital bed, Ajay sensed that his mother and father were quite different people. After his mother got off the phone, she always went to the cafeteria to get coffee for herself and Jell-O or cookies for him. He knew that if she took her coat with her it meant that she was especially sad. Instead of going directly to the cafeteria, she was going to go outside and walk around the hospital parking lot.

That day, while she was gone, Ajay stood beside the hospital bed and balanced a comic book on Birju's chest. He read to him very slowly. Before turning each page, he said, "OK, Birju?"

Birju was fourteen. He was thin and had curly hair. Immediately after the accident, there had been so many machines around his bed that only one person could stand beside him at a time. Now there was just a single waxy, yellow tube. One end of this went into his abdomen; the other, blocked by a green, bullet-shaped plug, was what his Isocal milk was poured through. When not being used, the tube was rolled up and bound by a rubber band and tucked beneath Birju's hospital gown. But even with the tube hidden it was obvious that there was something wrong with Birju. It was in his stillness and his open eyes. Once, in their house in Queens, Ajay had left a plastic bowl on a radiator overnight and the sides had drooped and sagged so that the bowl looked a little like an eye. Birju reminded Ajay of that bowl.

Ajay had not gone with his brother to the swimming pool on the day of the accident, because he had been reading a book and wanted to finish it. But he heard the ambulance siren from his aunt and uncle's house. The pool was only a few minutes away, and when he got there a crowd had gathered around the ambulance. Ajay saw his uncle first, in shorts and an undershirt, talking to a man inside the ambulance. His aunt was standing beside him. Then Ajay saw Birju on a stretcher, in blue shorts with a plastic mask over his nose and mouth. His aunt hurried over to take Ajay home. He cried as they walked, although he had been certain that Birju would be fine in a few days: in a Spider-Man comic he had just read, Aunt May had fallen into a coma and she had woken up perfectly fine. Ajay had cried simply because he felt crying was called for by the seriousness of the occasion. Perhaps this moment would mark the beginning of his future greatness. From that day on, Ajay found it hard to cry in front of his family. Whenever tears started coming, he felt like a liar. If he loved his brother, he knew, he would not have thought about himself as the ambulance had pulled away, nor would he talk with God at night about becoming famous.

When Ajay's mother returned to Birju's room with coffee and cookies, she sometimes talked to Ajay about Birju. She told him that when Birju was six he had seen a children's television show that had a character named Chunu, which was Birju's nickname, and he had thought the show was based on his own life. But most days Ajay went into the lounge to read. There was a TV in the corner and a lamp near a window that looked out over a parking lot. It was the perfect place to read. Ajay liked fantasy novels where the hero, who was preferably under the age of twenty-five, had an undiscovered talent that made him famous when it was revealed. He could read for hours without interruption, and sometimes when Vinod came to drive Ajay and his mother home from the hospital it was hard for him to remember the details of the real day that had passed.

One evening, when he was in the lounge, he saw a rock star being interviewed on *Entertainment Tonight*. The musician, dressed in a sleeveless undershirt that revealed a swarm of tattoos on his arms and shoulders, had begun to shout at the audience, over his interviewer, "Don't watch me! Live your life! I'm not you!" Filled with a sudden desire to do something, Ajay hurried out of the television lounge and stood on the sidewalk in front of the hospital entrance. But he did not know what to do. It was cold and dark and there was an enormous moon. Cars leaving the parking lot stopped one by one at the edge of the road. Ajay watched as they waited for an opening in the traffic, their brake lights glowing.

"ARE THINGS GETTING WORSE?" Ajay asked God. The weekend before had been Thanksgiving. Christmas would come soon, and a new year would start, a year during which Birju would not have talked or walked. Suddenly, Ajay understood hopelessness. Hopelessness felt very much like fear. It involved a clutching in the stomach and a numbness in the arms and legs.

"What do you think?" God answered.

"They seem to be."

"At least Birju's hospital hasn't forced him out."

"At least Birju isn't dead. At least Daddy's Greyhound bus has never skidded off a bridge." Lately, Ajay had begun talking much more quickly to God than he used to. Before, when he had talked to God, Ajay would think of what God would say in response before he said anything. Now, Ajay spoke without knowing how God might respond.

"You shouldn't be angry at me." God sighed. God was wearing his usual cardigan. "You can't understand why I do what I do."

"You should explain better then."

"Christ was my son. I loved Job. How long did Ram have to live in a forest?"

"What does that have to do with me?" This was usually the cue for discussing Ajay's prospects. But hopelessness made the future feel even more frightening than the present.

"I can't tell you what the connection is, but you'll be proud of yourself."

They were silent for a while.

"Do you love me truly?" Ajay asked.

"Yes."

"Will you make Birju normal?" As soon as Ajay asked the question, God ceased to be real. Ajay knew then that he was alone, lying under his blankets, his face exposed to the cold dark.

"I can't tell you the future," God said softly. These were words that Ajay already knew.

"Just get rid of the minutes when Birju lay on the bottom of the pool. What are three minutes to you?"

"Presidents die in less time than that. Planes crash in less time than that."

Ajay opened his eyes. His mother was on her side and she had a blanket pulled up to her neck. She looked like an ordinary woman. It surprised him that you couldn't tell, looking at her, that she had a son who was brain-dead.

IN FACT, THINGS WERE getting worse. Putting away his mother's mattress and his own in a closet in the morning, getting up very early so he could use the bathroom before his aunt or uncle did, spending so many hours in the hospital—all this had given Ajay the reassuring sense that real life was in abeyance, and that what was happening was unreal. He and his mother and brother were just waiting to make a long-delayed bus trip. The bus would come eventually to carry them to Queens, where he would return to school at P.S. 20 and to Sunday afternoons spent at the Hindi movie theater under the trestle for the 7 train. But now Ajay was starting to understand that the world was always real, whether you were reading a book or sleeping, and that it eroded you every day.

He saw the evidence of this erosion in his mother, who had

grown severe and unforgiving. Usually when Vinod brought her and Ajay home from the hospital, she had dinner with the rest of the family. After his mother helped his aunt wash the dishes, the two women watched theological action movies. One night, in spite of a headache that had made her sit with her eyes closed all afternoon, she ate dinner, washed dishes, sat down in front of the TV. As soon as the movie was over, she went upstairs, vomited, and lay on her mattress with a wet towel over her forehead. She asked Ajay to massage her neck and shoulders. As he did so, Ajay noticed that she was crying. The tears frightened Ajay and made him angry. "You shouldn't have watched TV," he said accusingly.

"I have to," she said. "People will cry with you once, and they will cry with you a second time. But if you cry a third time, people will say you are boring and always crying."

Ajay did not want to believe what she had said, but her cynicism made him think that she must have had conversations with his aunt and uncle that he did not know about. "That's not true," he told her, massaging her scalp. "Uncle is kind. Auntie Aruna is always kind."

"What do you know?" She shook her head, freeing herself from Ajay's fingers. She stared at him. Upside down, her face looked unfamiliar and terrifying. "If God lets Birju live long enough, you will become a stranger, too. You will say, 'I have been unhappy for so long because of Birju, now I don't want to talk about him or look at him.' Don't think I don't know you," she said.

Suddenly, Ajay hated himself. To hate himself was to see himself as the opposite of everything he wanted to be: short instead of tall, fat instead of thin. When he brushed his teeth that night, he looked at his face: his chin was round and fat as a heel. His nose was so broad that he had once been able to fit a small rock in one nostril.

His father was also being eroded. Before the accident, Ajay's father loved jokes—he could do perfect imitations—and Ajay had felt lucky to have him as a father. (Once, Ajay's father had convinced his own mother that he was possessed by the ghost of a British man.) And after the accident, his father had impressed Ajay with the patient loyalty of his weekly bus journeys. But now his father was different.

One Saturday afternoon, as Ajay and his father were returning from the hospital, his father slowed the car without warning and turned into the dirt parking lot of a bar that looked as though it had originally been a small house. It had a pitched roof with a black tarp. At the edge of the lot stood a tall neon sign of an orange hand lifting a mug of sudsy golden beer. Ajay had never seen anybody drink except in the movies. He wondered whether his father was going to ask for directions to somewhere, and if so, to where.

His father said, "One minute," and they climbed out of the car.

They went up wooden steps into the bar. Inside, it was dark and smelled of cigarette smoke and something stale and sweet. The floor was linoleum like the kitchen at his aunt and uncle's. There was a bar with stools around it, and a basketball game played on a television bolted against the ceiling, like the one in Birju's hospital room.

His father stood by the bar waiting for the bartender to notice him. His father had a round face and was wearing a white shirt and dark dress pants, as he often did on the weekend, since it was more economical to have the same clothes for the office and home.

The bartender came over. "How much for a Budweiser?" his father asked. It was a dollar fifty. "Can I buy a single cigarette?" He did not have to buy; the bartender would just give him one. His father helped Ajay up onto a stool and sat down himself. Ajay looked around and wondered what would happen if somebody started a knife fight. When his father had drunk half his beer, he carefully lit the cigarette. The bartender was standing at the end of the bar. There were only two other men in the place. Ajay was disappointed that there were no women wearing dresses slit all the way up their thighs. Perhaps they came in the evenings.

His father asked him if he had ever watched a basketball game all the way through.

"I've seen the Harlem Globetrotters."

His father smiled and took a sip. "I've heard they don't play other teams, because they can defeat everyone else so easily."

"They only play against each other, unless there is an emergency—like in the cartoon, when they play against the aliens to save the Earth," Ajay said.

"Aliens?"

Ajay blushed as he realized his father was teasing him.

When they left, the light outside felt too bright. As his father opened the car door for Ajay, he said, "I'm sorry."

That's when Ajay first felt that his father might have done something wrong. The thought made him worry. Once they were on the road, his father said gently, "Don't tell your mother."

Fear made Ajay feel cruel. He asked his father, "What do you think about when you think of Birju?"

Instead of becoming sad, Ajay's father smiled. "I am surprised by how strong he is. It's not easy for him to keep living. But, even before, he was strong. When he was interviewing for high school scholarships, one interviewer asked him, 'Are you a thinker or a doer?' He laughed and said, 'That's like asking, 'Are you an idiot or a moron?' "

From then on, they often stopped at the bar on the way back from the hospital. Ajay's father always asked the bartender for a cigarette before he sat down, and during the ride home he always reminded Ajay not to tell his mother.

Ajay found that he himself was changing. His superstitions were becoming extreme. Now when he walked around the good-luck tree he punched it, every other time, hard, so that his knuckles hurt. Afterward, he would hold his breath for a moment longer than he thought he could bear, and ask God to give the unused breaths to Birju.

IN DECEMBER, A PLACE opened in one of the good long-term care facilities. It was in New Jersey. This meant that Ajay and his mother could move back to New York and live with his father again. This was the news Ajay's father brought when he arrived for a two-week holiday at Christmas.

Ajay felt the clarity of panic. Life would be the same as before the accident but also unimaginably different. He would return to P.S. 20, while Birju continued to be fed through a tube in his abdomen. Life would be Birju's getting older and growing taller than their parents but having less consciousness than even a dog, which can become excited or afraid.

Ajay decided to use his devotion to shame God into fixing Birju. The fact that two religions regarded the coming December days as holy ones suggested to Ajay that prayers during this time would be especially potent. So he prayed whenever he thought of it—at his locker, even in the middle of a quiz. His mother wouldn't let him fast, but he started throwing away the lunch he took to school. And when his mother prayed in the morning, Ajay watched to make sure that she bowed at least once toward each of the postcards of deities. If she did not, he bowed three times to the possibly offended god on the postcard. He had noticed that his father finished his prayers in less time than it took to brush his teeth. And so now, when his father began praying in the morning, Ajay immediately crouched down beside him, because he knew his father would be embarrassed to get up first. But Ajay found it harder and harder to drift into the rhythm of sung prayers or into his nightly conversations with God. How could chanting and burning incense undo three minutes of a sunny August afternoon? It was like trying to move a sheet of blank paper from one end of a table to the other by blinking so fast that you started a breeze.

ON CHRISTMAS EVE, his mother asked the hospital chaplain to come to Birju's room and pray with them. The family knelt together beside Birju's bed. Afterward, the chaplain asked her whether she would be attending Christmas services. "Of course, Father," she said.

"I'm also coming," Ajay said.

The chaplain turned toward Ajay's father, who was sitting in a wheelchair because there was nowhere else to sit. "I'll wait for God at home," he said. That night, Ajay watched *It's a Wonderful Life* on television. To him, the movie meant that happiness arrived late, if ever. Later, when he got in bed and closed his eyes, God appeared. There was little to say.

"Will Birju be better in the morning?"

"No."

"Why not?"

"When you prayed for the math exam, you could have asked for Birju to get better and, instead of your getting an A, Birju would have woken."

This was so ridiculous that Ajay opened his eyes. His father was sleeping nearby on folded-up blankets. Ajay felt disappointed at not feeling guilt. Guilt might have contained some hope that God existed.

When Ajay arrived at the hospital with his father and mother the next morning, Birju was asleep, breathing through his mouth while a nurse poured a can of Isocal into his stomach through the yellow tube. Ajay had not expected that Birju would have recovered; nevertheless, seeing him that way put a weight in Ajay's chest.

The Christmas prayers were held in a large, mostly empty room; people in chairs sat next to people in wheelchairs. His father walked out in the middle of the service.

Later, Ajay sat in a corner of Birju's room and watched his parents. His mother was reading a Hindi women's magazine to Birju while she shelled peanuts into her lap. His father was reading a thick red book in preparation for a civil-service exam. The day wore on. The sky outside grew dark. At some point, Ajay began to cry. He tried to be quiet. He did not want his parents to notice his tears and think that he was crying for Birju, because in reality he was crying for how difficult his own life was.

His father noticed first. "What's the matter, hero?"

His mother shouted, "What happened?" and she sounded so alarmed it was as if Ajay were bleeding.

"I didn't get any Christmas presents! I need a Christmas present!" Ajay shouted. "You didn't buy me a Christmas present!" And then, because he had revealed his own selfishness, Ajay let himself sob. "You have to give me something. I should get something for all this." Ajay clenched his hands and wiped his face with his fists. "Each time I come here I should get something."

His mother pulled him up and pressed him into her stomach. His father came and stood beside them. "What do you want?" his father asked.

Ajay had no prepared answer for this. "What do you want?" his mother repeated.

The only thing he could think was, "I want to eat pizza and I want candy."

His mother stroked his hair and called him her little baby. She kept wiping his face with a fold of her sari. When at last he stopped crying, they decided that Ajay's father should take him back to his aunt and uncle's. On the way they stopped at a mini-mall. It was a little after five, and the streetlights were on. Ajay and his father did not take off their winter coats as they ate in a pizzeria staffed by Chinese people. While he chewed, Ajay closed his eyes and tried to imagine God looking like Clark Kent, wearing a cardigan and eyeglasses, but he could not. Afterward, Ajay and his father went next door to a magazine shop and Ajay got a bag of Three Musketeers bars and a bag of Reese's Peanut Butter Cups, and then he was tired and ready for home.

He held the candy in his lap while his father drove in silence. Even through the plastic, he could smell the sugar and chocolate. Some of the houses outside were dark, and others were outlined in Christmas lights.

After a while, Ajay rolled down the window slightly. The car filled with wind. They passed the building where Birju's accident had occurred. Ajay had not walked past it since the accident. When they drove by, he usually looked away. Now he tried to spot the fenced swimming pool at the building's side. He wondered whether the pool that had pressed itself into Birju's mouth and lungs and stomach had been drained, so that nobody would be touched by its unlucky waters. Probably it had not been emptied until fall. All summer long, people must have swum in the pool and sat on its sides, splashing their feet in the water, and not known that his brother had lain for three minutes on its concrete bottom one August afternoon.

WE DIDN'T LIKE HIM

We didn't like him. Manshu was fourteen, and we were eight or ten, and, instead of playing with boys his own age, he forced himself into our games. Often he came out into the lane and, if we were playing stick-stick, he'd say, "Give me the stick." Intimidated, we'd hand it over.

The lane had three- and four-story houses on both sides, so closely pressed together that the alley was always in shade. Once, we were playing cricket in the lane, Manshu batting. Nobody could get him out. The boy who was bowling, an eight-year-old, became angry and flung the ball away. Manshu twisted the boy's arm behind his back, forcing him to his knees. Then he gently tapped the top of the boy's head with the cricket bat, as if the boy were a wicket being driven into the ground.

Manshu was large, dark-skinned, round-faced. He was my

father's sister's husband's sister's son. Since he belonged to my aunt's husband's family, we had to show him the respect due to a family that takes a daughter away. The fact that I had to show deference was one more reason that he irritated me. And, because I was related to Manshu, the other boys treated me badly. They blamed me for his behavior, as if whatever he was doing were being done by my family.

Manshu's father had died when he was six. He lived with his mother in a large room on the second floor of an old house. The room had a high ceiling and blue-green walls. The nicest thing about it was that there was a swing hanging from the center of the ceiling.

Manshu's mother had diabetes and got tired very quickly. Many evenings, after she had gone to bed, Manshu would visit our house. When he came, he paid no attention to me. Instead, he addressed himself to my parents. He had a way of speaking that suggested that he understood other people's motivations. "Uncle," he said to my father once, "you know what Mrs. Kohli is like." When he spoke as if he knew things, I would think, Who are you to talk this way? Because I was eight and cruel, the way children are, I also thought, Why do you think you can talk when you don't even have a father?

My parents belonged to a generation that is mostly gone now, those very formal men and women who measured distance with *kos* and counted change in *annas*. When Manshu visited, my mother made him sherbet and presented it to him on a tray, which is the way she would have served it to an adult toward whom the family had to show formality.

My parents were polite with Manshu but periodically they said something that revealed that they found him and his mother irritating. Once, my mother told my father that everything Manshu said was probably a repetition of something his mother had uttered. Another time, when Manshu passed seventh standard and his mother went around the lane giving out boxes of sweets, my father said, "Surely he must have cheated."

Manshu's mother was always fainting. She would pass out in the lane, and some neighbor would come out and hold a glass of glucose water to her lips until she got up again. One day, when Manshu was sixteen, she fainted in the alley, but this time she didn't get up. For a while after she died, I did not believe that she was actually gone. A mother dying was the sort of thing that happened only in movies. I somehow imagined that Manshu's mother would come back in a few weeks, and that she would be angry when she returned. She would accuse people of disloyalty for having thought she could die.

Not long after her death, I went to Manshu's room with my parents. It smelled like it always had, of medicines and rubbing alcohol, of incense and cooking spices. The fact that nothing had changed felt wrong. It was confirmation that a horrible thing could occur and it would not matter. The fact that Manshu's misfortune could be ignored meant that I, too, might suffer misfortune and be treated this way. I got scared. I wanted to leave so badly that I did not care if I hurt Manshu's feelings.

MANSHU WAS HANDED OVER to my aunt's husband, who lived a few lanes away, but he continued to spend time in our lane. At first, I was embarrassed whenever I saw Manshu. He was quiet, meek. He appeared chastened. His curved shoulders would remind me that his mother was dead, and then I'd feel ashamed that I was more fortunate than he was.

Now, playing cricket with us, if he batted for a while and nobody could get him out, he would surrender the bat and let somebody else take a turn. This thoughtfulness may have been due to the fact that his uncle did not like him; Manshu felt that he had no one to take care of him so he was afraid of offending. It may also have come from the tenderness we all feel when someone we love dies.

Manshu began to visit the temple in our lane. The temple was narrow, with a marble-floored courtyard that had idols along all four sides and a tulsi bush in the center. In a larger temple, Manshu might have been able to sit quietly and be ignored, but Gaurji, the pandit, who lived on the second floor of the temple, saw it as his home. He did not like people to be there, other than for prayers. To him, they were intruding in his house. He would glower at the women who wanted to do service and came in the morning to wash the temple floor. Gaurji was irritable and slightly paranoid, as many pandits are, feeling that they are underpaid and not respected.

Manshu, because he was spending so much time at the temple, began to join Gaurji at each prayer. There were prayers in the morning, afternoon, evening, and night. During these, he sat right behind Gaurji. When Gaurji, bare-chested and skinny, his white dhoti wrapped around his narrow waist, rang his bell and blew on his shell, Manshu's high wavery voice stood out. My father was part of the committee that oversaw the temple, and Gaurji, of course, found it suspicious that somebody related to my father was spending so much time there, watching him. Once, Manshu asked to look at the prayer books and Gaurji began hitting him, slapping his face and shoulders. "What do you want?" he shouted. "At last, tell me what you want."

Manshu began to be religious. He was now seventeen or so. He stopped playing with us and started wearing sandalwood paste on his forehead. When he met somebody on the street, he said "*Ram, Ram*" instead of "*Namaste*." Manshu's religiosity became commonly known. Some women did their afternoon and evening prayers at home and liked to have another person present, because they felt that it would be more flattering to God to have two people praying than one. Manshu began to visit these women and sit before their altars as they sang. They would give him tea and crackers. My father found this embarrassing, as if Manshu were praying for food.

Manshu also bought some pamphlets on fortune-telling and astrology and started reading palms. He practiced at first on us children. We sat a step below him in the stairways of houses in the lane, our hands outstretched. When he read mine, I asked him whether I would be famous. "No," he said. This made me doubt that he could forecast the future.

He told me that I would own a dog and have problems with my knees.

MANSHU DID NOT do well in higher secondary. He was not able to get into college and so began studying for his B.Com. through correspondence school. He graduated in 1988. It is hard now to believe how difficult it was to get a job in India before 1991 and the economic liberalization. People would graduate from college, even good colleges, and remain unemployed for three or four years. Manshu became a tutor and continued living with his uncle.

I did not do especially well in higher secondary, either. I was able to get into law school, but it was a Hindi medium one, instead of one taught in English. While I was in law school, I came home regularly. It was strange to see Manshu still wandering the lanes, still going into people's homes to pray with them. He had grown a pandit's potbelly and he had a little Brahmin ponytail now. He wore slippers, instead of shoes, like someone who has to keep removing his footwear to enter sacred spaces. So much was changing in my life and so little in his that I began to see Manshu as simpleminded.

The difference between the late eighties and the mid-nineties was so great that it was as if there were decades separating them. When Manshu graduated from college, everyone wanted a government job. When I graduated from law school, everyone wanted to work for a foreign company. I was not smart enough to get a job with a multinational. I opened an office near the courts in Tis Hazari. It was a tin-roofed shed in a lane of tin-roofed sheds that were rented by lawyers. During the day, I'd walk up and down the lane, past tea stands and men sitting on stools beneath trees, typewriters before them. I talked to other lawyers, the fortunate ones in black gowns who were going to appear before a judge, and the rest of us, who wore dress pants and white shirts with pens in our breast pockets and kept our business cards rubber-banded in our pants pockets.

When I moved into the Tis Hazari office, I had a prayer ceremony performed in the shed. Manshu sat in the center of the cement room and lit a fire and soon the place was full of smoke and it was hard to breathe. Still, I sat there and sang prayers. Why not do something that might bring luck? Also, inviting the other lawyers in the lane to the prayer ceremony had been a way of getting to know people.

To cultivate business, I began helping my father with his volunteer work, which was how I started dealing with the committee that oversaw the temple.

No pandit ever wants to leave a temple. It is free housing and reasonable pay for not much effort. Also, one has an almost complete monopoly over the ceremonies held nearby in people's houses, and this can double or triple one's income. But Gaurji had a series of small strokes, and they made him even angrier. One winter evening, during prayers in the temple courtyard, he took the plates of food that had been put before the various gods for their dinner and began throwing them at the people who were seated cross-legged waiting for the prayers to start. I was sitting there when this occurred. He started calling us sister fuckers and ass sniffers. He stood before us, so angry that he was trembling. His eyes were dilated. I have only once or twice seen someone possessed, and seeing him, I had the same sense of astonishment I had when I witnessed a woman at Nizamuddin Dargah holding on to the marble jali, shouting "Mercy, mercy," as people chanted nearby.

Gaurji's youngest son wanted to replace his father; like me and Manshu, he had done badly in school. My father wanted to give the position to Manshu. He and the temple committee went to the temple and told the son that Manshu was going to be the new pandit.

The next morning, when the two old women who washed the temple floor arrived at the temple, the building's blue wooden doors were chained from the inside, the chains clanking whenever they tried to push them open.

The doors remained chained for several days. People walked past them and said angry things, before touching the steps that led into the temple and then bringing their hands to their foreheads.

Eventually, to drive out Gaurji and his family, we had to turn off the water and the electricity.

ALMOST IMMEDIATELY AFTER he became pandit, Manshu got married.

Manshu used to go on pilgrimages to Vaishno Devi three times a year. He returned from one of these with a non-Brahmin girl. He came back at night, entering the lane on foot because an auto rickshaw's rattle would have drawn too much attention. He must have been ashamed because he told no one in advance about the marriage and, even the next day, he did not visit us or his uncle to announce the news.

The girl was Vaishya, her family were merchants who sold firewood and coal, and my father became upset. He sat on a chair in our courtyard, his pajamas rolled up to his knees to sun his legs. "Always in his heart, I sensed there was selfishness," he said. "Now he's going to turn the temple into a business."

I tried to calm him. "I am a Brahmin, and I am as business minded as a Vaishya," I said.

I went to the temple to see Manshu. I agreed with my father that Manshu had behaved dishonestly, that he should have told us of his intention to marry out of caste before we made him pandit, but I was used to dealing with conflict by then, and I went calmly.

Manshu and I sat in one of the small rooms on the second floor, a low ceilinged room that was almost a cell.

"I knew you would not be angry," Manshu said immediately, as if to preempt whatever I might say.

"How can I be angry at your happiness?" I asked. I did not care that Manshu had married out of caste. It felt awkward, though, that he had done this while the knowledge that my family had supported him so strongly was still fresh in people's minds.

"Meet your sister-in-law," he said, and called out, "Aruna."

The woman who came through the door was short and round and fair-skinned. She looked like a Russian nesting doll. I got up and went and touched her feet. She gave a surprised laugh at being treated so formally. "Will you have tea?" she said.

Before I could answer, Manshu spoke. "She has diabetes, just like Ma." He was smiling and he said this almost proudly. His pride struck me as odd, and being reminded of his mother took me aback. Since I no longer thought of her, it had not occurred to me that she continued to be real to him.

After this, I treated Manshu and his wife the way I would a business contact. I dropped by the temple in the evenings to say hello. I made sure to tell people to use Manshu for prayer ceremonies, and I let him know that I was the one who had made the suggestion.

MY FATHER'S CONJECTURE about Manshu's plans for the temple turned out to be correct. One day, Manshu came to me. "How can I get on TV?" he asked, sitting on the other side of my desk. He wanted to be one of the yogis or miracle workers who are always on the cable channels. I didn't know. I said I guessed that you had to have a connection with someone who worked for the cable channels. He asked if I knew anyone like that. I did not.

Manshu then put an ad in *The Times of India*, a small box at the bottom of one of the middle pages, in which he claimed that praying at his temple might cure cancer. My mother said that he should go to jail. My father did not speak, only glowered.

For a few weeks, people came into the lane with the cut-out ad, asking for the temple.

I visited Manshu one evening soon after the ad had come out and asked him how effective it had been. We were standing in the temple courtyard. "You need a lot of money to make advertising work," Manshu said. "One or two ads is not enough." He said this angrily, as if his not having enough money for a lot of ads were some kind of injustice.

He put another ad in *The Times of India*. This time when people came to the temple courtyard with the cut-out ad, he performed miracles. He had learned some magic tricks and did such things as hold out an open palm before the visitor, close it, and then open it again to reveal blessed ashes.

Although the ads did not get him consistent new worshippers, they did help, in that he began to be asked to perform prayer ceremonies outside the neighborhood. Just the fact that he had been mentioned in the newspaper made him appear famous, and people liked having somebody famous pray for them.

The worst thing that Manshu did, in my eyes as well as in my father's, was start a small phone business at the end of the lane. Near the mouth of the lane, where it merges into a commercial street, were several shops, each about the size of a closet. One of these belonged to the temple. Originally, there had been an idol there so that people could pray on their way out of the lane to start their day. Gaurji, however, had convinced the temple committee that he needed more money, and his son had begun selling various knickknacks from there. Now Manshu put a phone in the closet and a curtain across it so that boys and girls who wanted to make friendship calls but did not want to use their cell phones could use the booth. It was improper for a pandit to be involved in this kind of business, but even worse was the fact that it was Manshu's wife who ran it. When a customer was in the booth, Aruna would come out into the lane and chatter with the other stall owners. She was popular with them for her willingness to be ordinary, but many of us felt that she was giving our lane a bad name.

IN THOSE DAYS, Manshu only rarely came to our house. He was busy and had his own family. My father, who did not actually want to see him, began to view his not visiting as disrespectful. It is hard to be around someone who has strong opinions without being influenced by those opinions. I, too, started to feel that Manshu was abusing us. I began to feel that he had tricked us, that he had taken advantage of our family relationship to become the pandit, and then had turned the temple into a business. I continued to see Manshu regularly, though, just as I continue to do business with people who strike me as immoral.

When my father was sixty-seven, the doctors told him that he had cancer. He went into the hospital for an operation, came out, and then had to go in again. He had chemotherapy, which caused his hair and his teeth to fall out. He became frail. His skin turned red, as if it were burned. Sometimes I sponge-bathed my father in his bed at home, patting him with a handkerchief, because a towel was too rough. Even the handkerchief could cause his skin to peel and bleed.

Near the end, he developed a lung infection. When I told him that I had to take him back to the hospital, he started to cry. "Why? What purpose will that serve?" he said, weeping.

I wanted him to keep living, though, so I told him that he was worrying for no reason. Because he was so afraid and lonely in his white room at the hospital, I asked everyone he knew to visit. I went to the temple several times to ask Manshu to visit. He did not come, though his wife did. I began to hate him around then.

I was with my father when he died. He was in his bed, open-eyed and hallucinating. "It's me. It's me," he said, right before he passed.

I took my father to Kanchi, the village by the Ganges where my family and many of the families in our lane perform cremations. As I walked around the pyre before it was lit and put the clarified butter on my father, I felt embarrassed, as if I were doing something wrong by putting butter on the nice silk kurta that he was wearing.

After the cremation, we asked Manshu to come to the house and lead the singing of the prayers. I did this because I wanted my father, even in death, not to be alone. I wanted him to be surrounded by people he knew. People came and sat cross-legged in the courtyard. Manshu sat on cushions in a corner, singing and playing a harmonium. His cell phone was lying on the cushion beside him, and periodically it would ring and he would gesture for us to keep singing while he answered the phone with one hand and played the harmonium with the other.

I was standing in a corner during the ceremony. It was a beautiful day and it was awful that my father was not there to see it. I also felt as though I were failing my father. He deserved more than he was receiving and I was not providing it.

I left the courtyard and went out into the lane. I walked toward the end of the alley. I was the only person there. As I walked, I panted. Halfway to the end of the lane, there was a scooter, and a cow eating some trash. I could hear the sound of the prayers from our house dying down, and this made me feel worse. I did not want the prayers to end, because once they were over all the rituals would be done and my father would somehow be more dead.

I came back to the courtyard and stood at the entrance. My mother was sitting near Manshu, her head covered with a fold of her white sari, rocking and weeping, surrounded by women, who were caressing her. Manshu looked up at me from his cushions and said, "Won't somebody say something about the soul that has left?"

I hate this eulogizing thing that has started up in India. To me, it is a Western fashion. Because of all these cable channels, pandits now watch American movies and they want to be seen as doing the latest, most advanced thing.

I remained silent in my corner.

"Will you let him go without saying anything?" Manshu said to the crowd. "Is he so little loved?"

One of my uncles, who was sitting on the floor near where I was standing, tapped my ankle.

I began speaking. "Ji, you all know what a kind man my father was. You know how he helped found orphanages." As I spoke, I began to sob. I felt angry that this intimate thing had been turned into a display. "You know that when my grandfather was dying, for two years he lay on his cot and my father took such good care of him that he never developed a bedsore."

I HATED MANSHU for years after that. I felt that he was pathologically selfish, that any decent person would have visited a dying relative, that any decent person would have tried to be humble during the funeral prayers instead of drawing attention to himself.

I stopped dropping by the temple. When we passed each other in the lane, I didn't speak to him.

Manshu's wife gave birth to two children, a girl named Priya and then, a few years later, a boy named Rahul. With her diabetes, she should not have had any. The girl was born without problems, but when Aruna gave birth to the boy she went into a coma. My mother went and sat in the temple with the many people from the lane who had come to pray for her.

Aruna woke from her coma but she remained unhealthy afterward. Years passed. Her black hair began to have white in it. She kept going in and out of the hospital. Manshu had bought a white van but he sold it to pay the hospital bills. Aruna still sometimes sat outside their phone booth. Other times they hired a neighborhood boy to oversee it. Eventually, she died.

Manshu was not close to his father's side of the family and so he asked me to help with the funeral. I had to do everything, from hiring the jeweler to come and snip the nose ring out of Aruna's nostril, to buying the coconuts and grass used in the prayers. Manshu did not have enough money for a wooden pyre.

I arranged the electric cremation. I arranged the jeep that took the body to the crematorium, and I hired a minibus to take people there. All the while I was doing this, I felt stupid for helping someone I hated.

Many people are vile. When I went with Manshu to pick up the ashes, the man who made us sign a register and gave them to us in a white cardboard box said that often people didn't bother to pick up their relatives' remains. "That is family love," he said, his eyes bloodshot, speaking with the bitterness typical of government employees.

Kanchi, where we were taking the ashes, is about a hundred kilometers from Delhi. I wanted to go directly there from the crematorium, but as we were getting into the car Manshu asked if we could first go back to the lane. He said that the children needed to salute their mother. It was a bright, hot day. I sighed loudly, obviously. I wanted to say no, to tell him that I did not have time to waste. Shame kept me from saying this, of course.

All the way back into the city, the traffic was stop-and-go. Manshu sat with the box in a red duffel bag in his lap. We parked opposite the mouth of the lane, with the busy street between us and the lane's entrance. Priya appeared, holding her brother's hand, and as she led him across the road, Manshu started sobbing. He got out of the car and left the bag on the seat and told his children to wait while he went and bought some flowers.

He left the car door open. I thought about closing it so that the air conditioning wouldn't escape. But it felt wrong to separate the children from their mother's ashes. Manshu returned.

He opened the bag's zipper so that we could see the box. "Say what I say," he said, and led them in a prayer, asking them to put handfuls of geraniums in the bag.

The drive to Kanchi took hours. At some point, Manshu fell asleep, his chin tipping into his chest. I looked at him as I drove and remembered my father's funeral ceremony, Manshu sitting in the corner talking on his cell phone. I felt that I was a fool, that I did not have the courage to take revenge.

Kanchi's primary industry is funerals. You get off the highway and almost immediately there is a parking lot. Along the lanes from the parking lot to the river there are only restaurants and flower shops. (The restaurants are there because for many families it is customary to eat a meal before they go back home.) The village's temples stand in a line by the river, and between them and the gray-green water is a steeply sloping sandy bank covered with shacks. Outside these, young men, Brahmins, in tight pants and cheap white shirts stand waiting.

Manshu sat on a cot beside one of these shacks, and a young man led him through the prayers. The cardboard box was open before him and there was a plastic bag inside, with ash and flecks of bone, like shards of seashell.

It was all depraved. In the middle of the prayers, the Brahmin turned to me, since I had been the one who selected him, and asked me to give him more money than we had agreed to. I told him that he had no shame. He said the next part of the prayer, so that Manshu could keep going, and then repeated that I needed to give more. We agreed on an amount, and then the prayers were finished.

Manshu and I walked down to the long wooden boats by the river. Several boatmen, short and wiry, came up to us as we reached the water. Again, as Manshu held the bag against his chest, there were nasty negotiations, with the boatmen demanding outrageous amounts. "Tell them that we need to go to the middle of the river," Manshu whispered. Often the boatmen stroke only a few yards from shore and demand that one pour one's ashes there. "You tell them," I wanted to say.

We got on one of the boats and the boatman poled us into the river. In the distance was a bridge, and on the other side were large buildings with chimneys. Manshu sat in the bow of the boat with the red duffel bag in his lap.

It was now mid-afternoon, and for a while there was only the creak of the pole in its lock and the splash of the water. Manshu sat there silently, the bag with its open cardboard box before him.

It was hot, and I was sweating heavily. The boatman pulled his pole out of the water and let us drift.

After a few minutes, he began stroking again so that we would not get caught by the current.

"Manshu, brother," I said, "you have to do it."

"She'll be all alone," Manshu murmured. "We won't be here and she'll be all alone."

I did not know what to say to this. I was sitting a few feet from him. I got up and crossed the boat. The boat tipped before me and the boatman moved from one side to the other. I took the box from the bag. "Let me help," I said. Manshu looked up at me, startled. I took out my car keys and used one to tear open the plastic bag. I held the bag out over the river with one hand and shook the ashes into the water. The bag lightened very quickly. Feeling it lighten, I realized that I was doing something wrong. When I had poured my father's ashes into the river, I had been glad that I was doing this for him, that I was taking care of him in this way. It was not fair to Aruna that someone outside her family was pouring her ashes into the river. It was not fair to Manshu that I was taking away this chance for him to care for his wife.

Once the bag was empty, I dipped it into the river and drained it so that all the ashes were gone. I flung the bag into the water. I threw the box also and the government form that said that the ashes were human remains.

NEAR KANCHI IS A VILLAGE famous for the deities that craftsmen there make out of clay and straw. They advertise their wares by standing the statues along the side of the road. We drove back to Delhi past half a mile of gods. In the car, holding the steering wheel, I could still feel the bag lightening in my hands. Not knowing what to say about the terrible thing I had done, I spoke to Manshu about the future. "You have to think of Priya and Rahul. They only have you now."

I parked the car by the mouth of our lane and phoned my mother and waited. After a few minutes, women began to appear at the entrance of the lane, carrying buckets. It is a ritual in our families that after putting someone in the Ganges, we bathe before we reenter the lane. Manshu and I got out of the car and took off our shoes and shirts. It was strange to feel the road beneath our bare feet and the hot polluted wind against our bellies. Then we tied towels around our waists and took off our pants and underwear. Scooters and bicycles stopped behind us and then slowly went around.

Before bathing myself, I bathed Manshu. I poured water on his head and then on his neck and back. I kneaded his fat shoulders. I rubbed his back with soap, his skin warm and the sun on my hands. I knelt down beside him and washed his legs and feet.

IF YOU SING LIKE THAT FOR ME

Late one June afternoon, seven months after my wedding, I woke from a short, deep sleep, in love with my husband. I did not know then, lying in bed and looking out the window at the line of gray clouds, that my love would last only a few hours and that I would never again care for Rajinder with the same urgency—never again in the five homes we would share and through the two daughters and one son we would also share, though unevenly and with great bitterness. I did not know this then, suddenly awake and only twenty-six, with a husband not much older, nor did I know that the memory of the coming hours would periodically overwhelm me throughout my life.

We were living in a small flat on the roof of a three-story house in Defense Colony, in New Delhi. Rajinder had signed the lease a week before our wedding. Two days after we married, he took me to the flat. I had thought I would be frightened entering my new home for the first time, but I was not. I felt very still that morning, watching Rajinder in his gray sweater bend over and open the padlock. Although it was cold, I wore only a pink silk sari and blouse, because I knew that my thick eyebrows, broad nose, and thin lips made me homely, and to win his love I must try especially hard to be appealing, even though I did not want to be.

The sun filled the living room through a window that took up half a wall and looked out onto the concrete roof. Rajinder went in first, holding the heavy brass padlock in his right hand. In the center of the room was a low plywood table with a thistle broom on top, and in a corner three plastic folding chairs lay collapsed on the floor. I followed a few steps behind Rajinder. The room was a white rectangle. Looking at it, I felt nothing. I saw the table and broom, the window grille with its drooping iron flowers, the dust in which we left our footprints, and I thought I should be feeling something, some anxiety, or fear, or curiosity. Perhaps even joy.

"We can put the TV there," Rajinder said softly, standing before the window and pointing to the right corner of the living room. He was slightly overweight and wore sweaters that were a bit large for him. They made him appear humble, a small man aware of his smallness. The thick black frames of his glasses, his old-fashioned mustache, as thin as a scratch, and the fading hairline created an impression of thoughtfulness. "The sofa before the window." At that moment, and often that day, I would think of myself with his smallness forever, bearing his children, going where he went, having to open always to his touch, and whatever I was looking at would begin to waver, and I would want to run. Run down the curving dark stairs, fast, fast, through the colony's narrow streets, with my sandals loud and alone, until I got to the bus stand and the 52 came, and then at the ice factory I would change to the 10, and finally I would climb the wooden steps to my parents' flat and the door would be open and no one would have noticed that I had gone with some small man.

I followed Rajinder into the bedroom, and the terror was gone, an open door now shut, and again I felt nothing, as if I were marble inside. The two rooms were exactly alike, except the bedroom was empty. "And there, the bed," Rajinder said, placing it with a slight wave of his hand against the wall across from the window. He spoke slowly and firmly, as if he were describing what was already there. "The fridge we can put right there," at the foot of the bed. Both were part of my dowry. Whenever he looked at me, I either said yes or nodded my head in agreement. We went outside and he showed me the kitchen and the bathroom, which were connected to the flat but could be entered only through doors opening onto the roof.

From the roof, a little after eleven, I watched Rajinder drive away on his scooter. He was going to my parents' flat in the Old Vegetable Market, where my dowry and our wedding gifts were stored. I had nothing to do while he was gone, so I wandered in and out of the flat and around the roof. Defense Colony was composed of rows of pale two- or three-story buildings. A small park, edged with eucalyptus trees, was behind our house.

Rajinder returned two hours later with his elder brother, Ashok, and a yellow van. It took three trips to bring the TV, the sofa, the fridge, the mixer, the steel plates, and my clothes. Each time they left, I wanted them never to return. Whenever they pulled up outside, Ashok pressed the horn, which played "Jingle Bells." I was frightened by Ashok, because, with his handlebar mustache and muscular forearms, he reminded me of my father's brothers, who, my mother claimed, beat their wives. Listening to his curses drift out of the stairwell each time he bumped against a wall while maneuvering the sofa, TV, and fridge up the stairs, I felt ashamed, as if he were cursing the dowry and, through it, me.

On the first trip they brought back two suitcases that my mother had packed with my clothes. I was cold, and when they left, I changed in the bedroom. My hands were trembling by then, and each time I swallowed, I felt a sharp pain in my throat that made my eyes water. Standing there in the room gray with dust, the light like cold, clear water, I felt sad and lonely and excited at being naked in an empty room in a place where no one knew me. I put on a salwar kameez, but even completely covered by the big shirt and pants, I was cold. I added a sweater and socks, but the cold had slipped under my skin and lingered beneath my fingernails.

Rajinder did not appear to notice I had changed. I swept the rooms while the men were gone, and stacked the kitchen shelves with the steel plates, saucers, and spoons that had come as gifts.

Rajinder and Ashok brought all the gifts except the bed, which was too big for them. It was raised to the roof by pulleys the next day. They were able to bring up the mattress, though, and the sight of it made me happy, for I knew I would fall asleep easily and that another eight hours would pass.

We did not eat lunch, but in the evening I made rotis and lentils on a kerosene stove. The kitchen had no lightbulb, and I had only the stove's blue flame to see by. The icy wind swirled around my feet. Nearly thirty years later I can still remember that wind. I could eat only one roti, while Rajinder and Ashok had six each. We sat in the living room, and they spoke loudly of their family's farm, gasoline prices, politics in Haryana, and Indira Gandhi's government. I spoke once, saying that I liked Indira Gandhi, and Ashok said that was because I was a Delhi woman who wanted to see women in power. My throat hurt and I felt as if I were breathing steam.

Ashok left after dinner, and Rajinder and I were truly alone for the first time since our marriage. Our voices were so respectful, we might have been in mourning. He took me silently in the bedroom, on the mattress beneath the window with the full moon peering in. When it was over and Rajinder was sleeping, I lifted myself on an elbow to look at him. I felt somehow that I could look at him more easily while he was asleep. I would not be nervous, trying to hide my scrutiny, and if the panic came, I could just hold on until it passed. I thought that if I could see him properly just once, I would no longer be frightened; I would know what kind of a man he was and what the future held. But the narrow mouth and the stiff, straight way he slept, with his arms folded across his chest, said one thing, and the long, dark eyelashes denied it. I stared at him until he started flickering, and then I closed my eyes.

Three months earlier, when our parents introduced us, I did not think we would marry. The neutrality of Rajinder's features, across the restaurant table from me, reassured me that we would not meet after that dinner. It was not that I expected to marry someone particularly handsome. I was neither pretty nor talented, and my family was not rich. But I could not imagine spending my life with someone so anonymous. If asked, I would have been unable to tell what kind of man I wanted to marry, whether he should be handsome and funny. I was not even certain I wanted to marry, though at times I thought marriage would make me less lonely. What I wanted was to be with someone who could make me different, someone other than the person I was.

Rajinder did not appear to be such a man, and although the fact that we were meeting meant that our families approved of each other, I still felt safe. Twice before, my parents had sat on either side of me as I met men found through the matrimonial section of the Sunday *Times of India*. One received a job offer in Bombay, and Ma and Pitaji did not want to send me that far away with someone they could not be sure of. The other, who was very handsome and drove a motorcycle, had lied about his income. I was glad that he had lied, for what could such a handsome man find in me?

Those two introductions were also held in Vikrant, a two-story dosa restaurant across from the Amba cinema. I liked Vikrant, for I thought the place's obvious cheapness would be held against us. The evening that Rajinder and I met, Vikrant was crowded with people waiting for the six-to-nine show. We sat down and an adolescent waiter swept bits of sambhar and dosa from the table onto the floor. Footsteps upstairs caused flecks of blue paint to drift down.

As the dinner began, Rajinder's mother, a small, round woman with a pockmarked face, spoke of her sorrow that Rajinder's father had not lived to see his two sons reach manhood. Ashok, sitting on one side of Rajinder, nodded slowly and solemnly at this. Rajinder gave no indication of what he thought. After a moment of silence Pitaji, obese and bald, tilted slightly forward and said, "It's all in the stars. What can a man do?" The waiter returned with five glasses of water, his fingers dipped to the second joint in the water. Rajinder and I were supposed to speak, but I was nervous, despite my certainty that we would not marry, and could think of nothing to say. We did not open our mouths until we ordered our dosas. Pitaji, worried that we would spend the meal in silence, asked Rajinder, "Other than work, how do you like to spend your time?" Then, to impress Rajinder with his sophistication, he added in English, "What hobbies you have?" The door to the kitchen, a few tables from us, was open, and I saw a cow standing near a skillet.

"I like to read the newspaper. In college I played badminton," Rajinder answered in English. His voice was respectful, and he smoothed each word with his tongue before letting go.

"Anita sometimes reads the newspapers," Ma said, and then became quiet at the absurdity of her words.

The food came and we ate quickly and mostly in silence,

though all of us made sure to leave a bit on the plate to show how full we were.

Rajinder's mother talked the most during the meal. She told us that Rajinder had always been favored over his older brother—a beautiful, hardworking boy who obeyed his mother like God Ram—and how Rajinder had paid her back by being the first in the family to leave the farm in Bursa to attend college, where he got a master's, and by becoming a bank officer. To get to work from Bursa he had to commute two and a half hours every day. This was very strenuous, she said, and Rajinder had long ago reached the age for marriage, so he wished to set up a household in the city. "We want a city girl," his mother said loudly, as if boasting of her modernity. "With an education but a strong respect for tradition."

"Asha, Anita's younger sister, is finishing her Ph.D. in molecular biology and might be going to America in a year, for further studies," Ma said slowly, almost accidentally. She was a short, dark woman, so thin that her skin hung loose. "Two of my brothers are doctors; so is one sister. And I have one brother who is an engineer. I wanted Anita to be a doctor, but she was lazy and did not study." My mother and I loved each other, but sometimes something inside her would slip, and she would attack me, and she was so clever and I loved her so much that all I could do was feel helpless.

Dinner ended and I still had not spoken. When Rajinder said he did not want any dessert, I asked, "Do you like movies?" It was the only question I could think of, and I had felt pressured by Pitaji's stares.

"A little," Rajinder said seriously. After a pause he asked, "And you, do you like movies?"

"Yes," I said, and then, to be daring and to assert my personality, I added, "very much."

TWO DAYS AFTER that Pitaji asked me if I would mind marrying Rajinder, and because I could not think of any reason not to, I said all right. Still, I did not think we would marry. Something would come up. His family might decide that my B.A. and B.Ed. were not enough, or Rajinder might suddenly announce that he was in love with his typist.

The engagement occurred a month later, and although I was not allowed to attend the ceremony, Asha was, and she described everything. Rajinder sat cross-legged before the pandit and the holy fire. Pitaji's pants were too tight for him to fold his legs, and he had to keep a foot on either side of the fire. Ashok and his mother were on either side of Rajinder. The small pink room was crowded with Rajinder's aunts and uncles. The uncles, Asha said, were unshaven and smelled faintly of manure. The pandit chanted in Sanskrit and at certain points motioned for Pitaji to tie a red thread around Rajinder's right wrist and to place a packet of one hundred five-rupee bills in his lap.

Only then, as Asha, grinning, described the ceremony, did I realize that I would actually marry Rajinder. I was shocked. I seemed to be standing outside myself, a stranger, looking at two women, Anita and Asha, sitting on a brown sofa in a wide, bright room. We were two women, both of whom would cry if slapped, laugh if tickled. But one was doing her Ph.D. and possibly going to America, and the other, her elder sister, who was slow in school, was now going to marry and have children and grow old. Why will she go to America and I stay here? I wanted to demand of someone, anyone. Why, when Pitaji took us out of school, saying what good was education for girls, did Asha, then only in third grade, go and re-enroll herself, while I waited for Pitaji to change his mind? I felt so sad I could not even hate Asha for her thoughtlessness.

As the days until the wedding evaporated, I had difficulty sleeping, and sometimes everything was lost in a sudden brightness. Often I woke at night and thought the engagement was a dream. Ma and Pitaji mentioned the marriage only in connection with the shopping involved. Once, Asha asked what I was feeling about the marriage, and I said, "What do you care?"

When I placed the necklace of marigolds around Rajinder's neck, to seal our marriage, I brushed my hand against his neck to confirm the reality of his presence. The pandit recited Sanskrit verses, occasionally pouring clarified butter into the holy fire, which we had just circled seven times. It is done, I thought. I am married now. I felt no different. I was wearing a bright red silk sari and could smell the sourness of new cloth. People were surrounding us, many people. Movie songs blared over the loudspeakers. On the ground was a red-and-black-striped carpet. The tent above us had the same stripes. Rajinder draped a garland around my neck and everyone began cheering. Their voices smothered the rumble of the night's traffic passing on the road outside the alley.

Although the celebration lasted another six hours, ending at about one in the morning, I did not remember most of it until many years later. I did not remember the two red thrones on which we sat and received the congratulations of women in pretty silk saris and men wearing handsome pants and shirts. I know about the cold only because of the photos showing vapor coming from people's mouths as they spoke. I still do not remember what I thought as I sat there. For nearly eight years I did not remember Ashok and his mother, Ma, Pitaji, and Asha getting in the car with us to go to the temple hostel where the people from Rajinder's side were housed. Nor did I remember walking through the long halls, with moisture on the once-white walls, and seeing in rooms, long and wide, people sleeping on cots, mattresses without frames, blankets folded twice before being laid down. I did not remember all this until one evening eight years later, while wandering through Kamla Nagar market searching for a dress for Asha's first daughter. I was standing on the sidewalk looking at a stall display of hairbands and thinking of Asha's husband, a tall, yellow-haired American with a soft, open face, who I felt had made Asha happier and gentler. And then I began crying. People brushed past, trying to ignore me. I was so alone. I was thirty-three years old and so alone that I wanted to sit down on the sidewalk until someone came and picked me up.

I did remember Rajinder's opening the blue door to the room where we would spend our wedding night. Before we entered, we separated for a moment. Rajinder touched his mother's feet with his right hand and then touched his forehead with that hand. His mother embraced him. I did the same with each of my parents. As Ma held me, she whispered, "Earlier your father got drunk like the pig he is." Then Pitaji put his arms around me and said, "I love you," in English.

The English was what made me cry, even though everyone thought it was the grief of parting. The words reminded me of how Pitaji came home drunk after work once or twice a month and Ma, thin arms folded across her chest, stood in the doorway of his bedroom and watched him fumbling to undress. When I was young, he held me in his lap those nights, his arm tight around my waist, and spoke into my ear in English, as if to prove that he was sober. He would say, "No one loves me. You love me, don't you, my little sun-ripened mango? I try to be good. I work all day, but no one loves me." As he spoke, he rocked in place. He would be watching Ma to make sure she heard. Gradually his voice would become husky. He would cry slowly, gently, and when the tears began to come, he would let me go and continue rocking, lost gratefully in his own sadness. Sometimes he turned out the lights and cried silently in the dark for a half hour or more. Then he locked the door to his room and slept.

Those nights Ma offered dinner without speaking. Later she told her own story. But she did not cry, and although Ma knew how to let her voice falter as if the pain were too much to speak of, and her face crumpled with sorrow, I was more impressed by Pitaji's tears. Ma's story included some beautiful lines. Lines like "In higher secondary a teacher said, 'In seven years all the cells in our body change.' So when Baby died, I thought, It will be all right. In seven years none of me will have touched Baby." Other lines were as fine, but this was Asha's favorite. It might have been what first interested her in microbiology. Ma would not eat dinner, but she sat with us on the floor and, leaning forward, told us how she had loved Pitaji once, but after Baby got sick and she kept sending telegrams to Beri for Pitaji to come home and he did not, she did not send a telegram about Baby's death. "What could he do," she would say, looking at the floor, "although he always cries so handsomely?" I was dazzled by her words—calling his tears handsome—in comparison with which Pitaji's ramblings appeared inept. But the grief of the tears seemed irrefutable. And because Ma loved Asha more than she did me, I was less compassionate toward her. When Pitaji awoke and asked for water to dissolve the herbs and medicines he took to make himself vomit, I obeyed readily. When Pitaji spoke of love on my wedding night, the soft, wet vowels of his vomiting were what I remembered.

Rajinder closed and bolted the door. A double bed was in the corner of the room and near it a small table with a jug of water and two glasses. The room had yellow walls and smelled faintly of mildew. I stopped crying and suddenly felt very calm. I stood in the center of the room, a fold of the sari covering my head and falling before my eyes. I thought, I will just say this has been a terrible mistake. Rajinder lifted the sari's fold and, looking into my eyes, said he was very pleased to marry me. He was wearing a white silk kurta with tiny flowers embroidered around the neck and gold studs for buttons. He led me to the bed with his hand on my elbow and with a light squeeze let me know he wanted me to sit. He took off the loose shirt and suddenly looked small. *No, wait. I must tell you,* I said. His stomach drooped. What an ugly man, I thought. *No. Wait,* I said. He did not hear or I did not say. Louder. *You are a very nice man, I am sure.* The hard bed with the white sheet dotted with rose petals. The hands that undid the blouse and were disappointed by my small breasts. The ceiling was so far away. The moisture between my legs like breath on glass. Rajinder put his kurta back on and poured himself some water and then thought to offer me some.

Sleep was there, cool and dark, as soon as I closed my eyes. But around eight in the morning, when Rajinder shook me awake, I was exhausted. The door to our room was open, and I saw one of Rajinder's cousins, a fat, hairy man with a towel around his waist, walk past to the bathroom. He looked in and smiled broadly, and I felt ashamed. I was glad I had gotten up at some point in the night and wrapped the sari on again. I had not felt cold, but I had wanted to be completely covered.

Rajinder, Ashok, their mother, and I had breakfast in our room. We sat around the small table and ate rice and yogurt. I wanted to sleep. I wanted to tell them to go away, to stop talking about who had come last night and brought what, and who had not but might still be expected to send a gift, tell them they were boring, foolish people. Ashok and his mother spoke, while Rajinder just nodded. Their words were indistinct, as if coming from across a wide room, and I felt I was dreaming them. I wanted to close my eyes and rest my head on the table. "You eat like a bird," Rajinder's mother said, looking at me and smiling.

After breakfast we visited a widowed aunt of Rajinder's who had been unable to attend the wedding because of arthritis. She lived in a two-room flat covered with posters of gods and smelling of mothballs and old sweat. As she spoke of how carpenters and cobblers were moving in from the villages and passing themselves off as upper-castes, she drooled from the corners of her mouth. I was silent, except for when she asked me about my education and what dishes I liked to cook. As we left, she said, "A thousand years. A thousand children," and pressed fifty-one rupees into Rajinder's hands.

Then there was the long bus ride to Bursa. The roads were so bad that I kept being jolted awake, and my sleep became so fractured that I dreamed of the bus ride and being awakened. And in the village I saw grimy hens peering into the well, and women for whom I posed demurely in the courtyard. They sat in a circle around me and murmured compliments. My head and eyes were covered as they had been the night before, and as I stared at the floor, I fell asleep. I woke an hour later to their praise of my modesty. That night, in the dark room at the rear of the house, I was awakened by Rajinder's digging between my legs, and although he tried to be gentle, I just wished it over. His face, flat and distorted, was above me, and his hands raised my nipples cruelly, resentful of being cheated, even though I never heard anger in Rajinder's voice. He was always polite. Even in bed he was formal. "Could you get on all fours, please?"

⁂

SO HEAVY AND STILL did I feel on the first night in our new rooftop home, watching Rajinder sleep on the moonlight-soaked mattress, that I wanted the earth and sky to stop turning and for it always to be night. I did not want dawn to come and the day's activities to start again. I did not want to have to think and react to the world. I fell asleep then, only to wake in panic an hour later at the thought of the obscure life I would lead with Rajinder. Think slowly, I told myself, looking at Rajinder asleep with an arm thrown over his eyes. Slowly. I remembered the year between my B.A. and B.Ed., when, through influence, I got a job as a typist in a candle factory. For nearly a month, upon reaching home after work, I wanted to cry, for I was terrified at the idea of giving up eight hours a day, a third of my life, to typing letters concerning supplies of wax. And then one day I noticed that I no longer felt afraid. I had learned to stop thinking. I floated above the days.

In the morning I had a fever, and the stillness it brought with it spread into the coming days. It hardened around me, so that I did not feel as if I were the one making love or cooking dinner or going home to see Ma and Pitaji and behaving there as I always had. No one guessed it was not me. Nothing could break through the stillness, not even Rajinder's learning to caress me before parting my legs, or my growing to know all the turns of the colony's alleys and the shopkeepers calling me by name.

⁂

WINTER TURNED INTO spring, and the trees in the park swelled green. Rajinder was thoughtful and generous. Traveling for conferences to Baroda, Madras, Jaipur, Bangalore, he always brought back saris or other gifts. The week I had malaria, he came home every lunch hour and cooked gruel for me. On my twenty-sixth birthday he took me to the Taj Mahal, and arranged for my family to be hidden in the flat when we returned in the evening. What a good man, I thought then, watching him standing proudly in a corner. What a good man, I thought, and was frightened, for that was not enough. I knew I needed something else, but I did not know what. Being his wife was not so bad. He did not make me do anything I did not want to, except make love, and even that was sometimes pleasant. I did not mind his being in the flat, and being alone is difficult. When he was away on his trips, I did not miss him, and he, I think, did not miss me, for he never mentioned it.

Summer came, and hot winds swept up from the Rajasthani deserts. The old cows that wander unattended on Delhi's streets began to die. The corpses lay untouched for a week sometimes; their tongues swelled and, cracking open the jaw, stuck out absurdly.

The heat was like a high-pitched buzzing that formed a film between flesh and bone, so that my skin felt thick and rubbery and I wished that I could just peel it off. I woke at four every morning to have an hour when breathing air would not be like inhaling liquid. By five the eastern edge of the sky was too bright to look at, even though the sun had yet to appear. I bathed both before and after breakfast and again after doing laundry but before lunch. As June progressed, and the very air seemed to whine under the heat's stress, I stopped eating lunch. Around two, before taking my nap, I would pour a few mugs of water on my head. I liked to lie on the bed imagining that the monsoon had come. Sometimes this made me sad, for the smell of wet earth and the sound of rain have always made me feel as if I have been waiting for someone all my life and that person has not yet come. I dreamed often of living near the sea, in a house with a sloping red roof and bright blue window frames, and woke happy, hearing water on sand.

And so the summer passed, slowly and vengefully, until the last week of June, when *The Times of India* began its countdown to the monsoon, and I woke one afternoon in love with my husband.

I HAD RETURNED home that day after spending two weeks with my parents. Pitaji had had a mild heart attack, and I took turns with Ma and Asha being with him in Safdarjung Hospital. The heart attack was no surprise, for Pitaji had become so fat that even his largest shirts had to be worn unbuttoned. So when I opened the door late one night and saw Asha with her fist up, ready to start banging again, I did not have to be told that Pitaji had woken screaming that his heart was breaking.

While I hurried a sari and blouse into a plastic bag, Asha leaned against a wall of our bedroom, drinking water. It was three. Rajinder, in his undershirt and pajama pants, sat on the bed's edge and stared at the floor. I felt no fear, perhaps because Asha had said the heart attack was not so bad, or perhaps because I just did not care. The rushing and the banging on the doors appeared to be the properly melodramatic behavior when one's father might be dying.

An auto rickshaw was waiting for us downstairs, triangular, small, with plasticized cloth covering its frame. It seemed like a vehicle for desperate people. Before getting in, I looked up and saw Rajinder. He was leaning against the railing. The moon was yellow and uneven behind him. I waved and he waved back. Such formalities, I thought, and then we were off, racing through dark, abandoned streets.

"Ma's fine. He screamed so loud," Asha said. She is a few inches taller than I am, and although she too is not pretty, she uses makeup that gives angles to her round face. Asha sat slightly turned on the seat so that she could face me. "A thousand times we told him, lose weight," she said, shaking her head impatiently. "When the doctor gave him that diet, he said, 'Is that before or after breakfast?'" She paused and added in a tight whisper, "He's laughing now."

I felt lonely sitting there while the city was silent and dark and we talked of our father without concern. "He wants to die," I said softly. I enjoyed saying such serious words. "He is so unhappy. I think our hopes are made when we are young, and we can never adjust them to the real world. He was nearly national champion in wrestling, and for the last thirty-seven years he has been examining government schools to see that they have the right PE equipment. He loves eating, and that is as fine a way to die as any."

"If he wants to die, wonderful; I don't like him. But why is he making it difficult for us?"

Her directness shocked me and made me feel that my sentimentality was dishonest. The night air was still bitter from the evening traffic. "He is a good man," I said unsteadily.

"The way he treated us all. Ma is like a slave."

"They are just not good together. It's no one's fault."

"How can it be no one's fault?"

"His father was an alcoholic."

"How long can you use your parents as an excuse?"

I did not respond at first, for I thought Asha might be saying this because I had always used Ma and Pitaji to explain away my failures. Then I said, "Look how good he is compared with his brothers. He must have had something good inside that let him be gentler than them. We should love him for that part alone."

"That's what he is relying on. It's a big world. A lot of people are worth loving. Why love someone mediocre?"

Broken glass was in the hallways of the hospital, and someone had urinated in the elevator. When we came into the yellow room that Pitaji shared with five other men, he was asleep. His face looked like a shiny brown stone. He was on the bed nearest the window. Ma sat at the foot of his bed, her back to us, looking out at the fading night.

"He will be all right," I said.

Turning toward us, Ma said, "When he goes, he wants to make sure we all hurt." She was crying. "I thought I did not love him, but you can't live this long with a person and not love just a bit. He knew that. When they were bringing him here, he said, 'See what you have done, demoness?' "

Asha took Ma away, still crying. I spent the rest of the night dozing next to his bed.

We fell into a pattern. Ma usually came in the morning, around eight, and I replaced her, hours later. Asha would take my place at three and stay until six, and then Ma's brother or his sons would stay until Ma returned.

I had thought I would be afraid of being in the hospital, but it was very peaceful. Pitaji slept most of every day and night because of the medicines, waking up every now and then to ask for water and quickly falling asleep again. A nice boy named Rajeeve, who also was staying with his father, told me funny stories about his family. At night Asha and I slept on adjacent cots on the roof. Before she went to bed, she read five pages of an English dictionary. She had been accepted into a postdoctoral program in America. She did not brag about it as I would have. Like Ma, Asha worked very hard, as if that were the only way to live and one needn't talk about it, and as if, like Ma, she assumed that we were all equally fortunate. But sometimes Asha would shout a word at me—"Alluvial"—and then look at me as if she was waiting for a response. Once, Rajinder came to drop off some clothes, but I was away. I did not see him or talk with him for the two weeks.

Sometimes Pitaji could not sleep and he would tell me stories of his father, a schoolteacher, who would take Pitaji with him to the saloon, so that someone would be there to guide him home when he was drunk. Pitaji was eight or nine then. His mother beat him for accompanying Dadaji, but Pitaji, his breath sounding as if it were coming through a wet cloth, said that he was afraid Dadaji would be made fun of if he walked home alone. Pitaji told the story quietly, as if he were talking about someone else, and as soon as he finished, he changed the subject. I could not tell whether Pitaji was being modest or was manipulating me by pretending to be modest.

He slept most of the day, and I sat beside him, listening to his little green transistor radio. The June sun filled half the sky, and the groundskeeper walked around the courtyard of the hospital in wide circles with a water bag as large as a man's body slung over one shoulder. He was sprinkling water to keep the dust settled. Sometimes I hummed along to Lata Mangeshkar or Mohammed Rafi singing that grief is no letter to be passed around to whoever wants to read.

There were afternoons when Pitaji became restless and whispered conspiratorially that he had always loved me most. Watching his face, puffy from the drugs, his nose broad and covered with blackheads, as he said again that Ma did not talk to him or that Asha was indifferent to his suffering, I felt exhausted. When he complained to Asha, "Your mother doesn't talk to me," she answered, "Maybe you aren't interesting."

Once, four or five days before we took him home, as he was complaining, I got up from the chair and went to look out the window. Beyond the courtyard was a string of yellow-and-black auto rickshaws waiting under eucalyptus trees. I wanted desperately for Asha to come, so that I could leave, and bathe, and lie down to dream of a house with a red-tiled roof near the sea.

"You must forgive me," Pitaji said as I looked out the window. I was surprised, for I could not remember his ever apologizing. "I sometimes forget that I will die soon and so act like a man who has many years left." I felt frightened, for I suddenly wanted to love him but could not trust him enough.

From then until we went home, Pitaji spoke little. Once, I forgot to bring his lunch from home and he did not complain, whereas before he would have screamed and tried to make me feel guilty. A few times he began crying to himself for no reason, and when I asked why, he did not answer.

Around eleven the day Pitaji was released, an ambulance carried Ma, Pitaji, and me to the Old Vegetable Market. Two orderlies, muscular men in white uniforms, carried him on a stretcher up three flights of stairs into the flat. The flat had four rooms and was part of a circle of dilapidated buildings that shared a courtyard. Fourteen or fifteen people turned out to watch Pitaji's return. Some of the very old women, sitting on cots in the courtyard, asked who Pitaji was, although he had lived there for twenty years. A few children climbed into the ambulance and played with the horn until they were chased out.

The orderlies laid Pitaji on the cot in his bedroom and left. The room was small and dark, smelling faintly of the kerosene with which the bookshelves were treated every other week to prevent termites. Traveling had tired him, and he fell asleep quickly. He woke as I was about to leave. Ma and I were speaking in whispers outside his bedroom.

"I am used to his screaming," Ma said. "He won't get any greasy food here. But once he can walk . . ."

"He seems to have changed."

"Right now he's afraid. Give him a few days and he'll return to normal. People can't change, even if they want to."

"What are you saying about me?" Pitaji tried to call out, but his voice was like wind on dry grass.

"You want something?" Ma asked.

"Water."

As I started toward the fridge, Ma said, "Nothing cold." The clay pot held only enough for one glass. I knelt beside the cot and helped Pitaji rise to a forty-five-degree angle. His heaviness and the weakness of his body moved me. Like a baby holding a bottle, Pitaji held the glass with both hands and made sucking noises as he drank. I lowered him when his shoulder muscles slackened. His eyes were red, and they moved about the room slowly. I wondered whether I could safely love him if I did not reveal my feelings.

"More?" he asked.

"Only fridge water," I said. Ma was clattering in the kitchen. "I am going home."

"Rajinder is good?" He looked at the ceiling while speaking. "Yes," I said. A handkerchief of light covered his face, and faint blue veins, like delicate, almost translucent roots, showed through the skin of his forehead. "The results for his exam came," I told him. "He will be promoted. He was second in Delhi." Pitaji closed his eyes. "Are you hurting?" I asked.

"I feel tired."

I, too, felt tired. I did not know what to do with my new love or whether it would last. "That will pass, the doctor said. Why don't you sleep?"

"I don't want to," he said loudly, and my love drew back.

"I must go," I said, but made no move to.

"Forgive me," he said, and again I was surprised. "I am not worried usually, but I get frightened sometimes. Sometimes I dream that the heaviness is dirt. What an awful thing to be a Muslim or a Christian." He spoke slowly, and I felt my love returning. "Once, I dreamed of Baby's ghost."

"Oh."

"He was eight or nine and did not recognize me. He did not look like me. I was surprised, because he was my son and I had always expected him to look like me."

I felt exhausted. Something about the story was both awkward and polished, which indicated deceit. But Pitaji never lied completely, and the tiring part was not knowing. "God will forgive you," I said. But why should he? I thought. Why do people always think hurting others is all right, as long as they hurt themselves as well?

"Your mother has not."

I placed my hand on his, knowing that I was already in the trap. "Shhh."

"At your birthday, when she sang, I said, 'If you sing like that for me every day, I will love you forever.'"

"She loves you. She worries about you."

"That's not the same. When I tell Asha this, she tells me I'm sentimental. Ratha loved me once. But she cannot forgive.

What happened so long ago, she cannot forgive." He was blinking rapidly, preparing to cry. "But that is a lie. She does not love me because"—and he began crying without making a sound—"I did not love her for so long."

"Shhh. She loves you. She was just saying, 'Oh, I love him so. I hope he gets better, for I love him so.' "

"Ratha could have loved me a little. She could have loved me twenty for my eleven." He was sobbing.

"Shhh. Shhh. Shhh." I wanted to run away, far away, and be someone else.

THE SLEEP THAT AFTERNOON was like falling. I lay down, closed my eyes, and plummeted. I woke as suddenly, without any half memories of dreams, into a silence that meant that the power was gone, and the ceiling fan was still, and the fridge was slowly warming,

It was cool, I noticed, unsurprised by the monsoon's approach—for I was in love. The window curtains stirred, revealing TV antennas and distant gray clouds and a few sparrows wheeling in the air. The sheet lay bunched at my feet. I felt gigantic. My legs stretched thousands of miles; my head rested in the Himalayas and my breath brought the world rain. If I stood up, I would scrape against the sky. But I was small and compact and distilled, too. I am in love, I thought, and a raspy voice echoed the words in my head, causing me to panic and lose my sense of omnipotence for a moment. I will love

Rajinder slowly and carefully and cunningly, I thought, and suddenly felt peaceful again, as if I were a lake and the world could only form ripples on my surface, while the calm beneath continued in solitude. Time seemed endless, and I would surely have the minutes and seconds needed to plan a method of preserving this love, like the feeling in your stomach when you are in a car going swiftly down a hill. Don't worry, I thought, and I no longer did. My mind obeyed me limply, as if a terrible exhaustion had worn away all rebellion.

I got up and swung my legs off the bed. I was surprised that my love was not disturbed by my physical movements. I walked out onto the roof. The wind ruffled the treetops and small, gray clouds slid across the cool, pale sky. On the street, eight or nine young boys played cricket. The school year had just started, and the children played desperately, as if they must run faster, leap higher, to recapture the hours spent indoors.

Tell me your stories, I would ask him. Pour them into me, so that I know everything you have ever loved or been scared of or laughed at. But thinking this, I became uneasy and feared that when I actually saw him, my love would fade and I would find my tongue thick and unresponsive. What should I say? I woke this afternoon in love with you. I love you too, he would answer. No, no, you see, I really love you. I love you so much that I think anything is possible, that I will live forever. Oh, he would say, and I would feel my love rush out of me.

I must say nothing at first, I decided. Slowly I will win his love. I will spoil him, and he will fall in love with me. And as long as he loves me, I will be able to love him. I will love him like a camera that closes at too much light and opens at too little, so his blemishes will never mar my love.

I watched the cricket game to the end. I felt very happy standing there, as if I had just discovered some profound secret. When the children dispersed, around five, I knew Rajinder would be home soon.

I bathed and changed into new clothes. I stood before the small mirror in the armoire as I dressed. Uneven brown aureoles, a flat stomach, the veins in my feet like pen marks. Will this be enough? I wondered. Once he loves me, I told myself. I lifted my arms and tried to smell the plantlike odor of my perspiration. I wore a bright-red cotton sari. What will I say first? *Namaste*—How was your day? With the informal "you." How was your day? The words felt strange, for I had never before used the informal with him. I had, as a show of modesty, never even used his name, except on the night before my wedding, when I said it over and over to myself to see how it felt—like nothing. Now when I said "Rajinder," the three syllables had too many edges, and again I doubted that he would love me. "Rajinder, Rajinder," I said rapidly several times, until it no longer felt strange. He will love me because to do otherwise would be too lonely, because I will love him so. I heard a scooter stopping outside the building and knew that he had come home.

My stomach was small and hard as I walked onto the roof. The dark clouds made it appear as if it were seven instead of five thirty. I saw him roll the scooter into the courtyard and I felt happy. He parked the scooter and took off his gray helmet. He combed his hair carefully to hide the growing bald spot. The deliberateness of the way he tucked the comb into his back pocket overwhelmed me with tenderness. We will love each other gently and carefully, I thought.

I waited for him to rise out of the stairwell. The wind made my petticoat, drying on the clothesline, go *clap, clap*. I was smiling rigidly. How was your day? How was your day? Was your day good? Don't be so afraid, I told myself. What does it matter how you say hello? Tomorrow will come, and the day after, and the day after that.

His steps sounded like a shuffle. Leather rubbing against stone. Something forlorn and steady in the sound made me feel as if I were twenty years older and this were a game I should stop or I might get hurt. Rajinder, Rajinder, Rajinder, how are you?

First the head: oval, high forehead, handsome eyebrows. Then the not so broad but not so narrow shoulders. The top two buttons of the cream shirt were opened, revealing an undershirt and some hair. The two weeks had not changed him, yet seeing him, I felt as if he were somehow different, denser.

"How was your day?" I asked him, while he was still in the stairwell.

"All right," he said, stepping onto the balcony. He smiled, and I felt happy. His helmet was in his left hand and he had a plastic bag of mangoes in his right. "When did you get home?" The "you" was informal, and I felt a surge of relief. He will not resist, I thought.

"A little after three."

I followed him into the bedroom. He placed the helmet on the windowsill and the mangoes in the refrigerator. His careful way of folding the plastic bag before placing it in the basket on top of the refrigerator moved me.

"Your father is fine?"

I did not say anything.

Rajinder walked to the sink on the outside bathroom wall.

I stood in the bedroom doorway and watched him wash his hands and face with soap. Before putting the chunk of soap down, he rinsed it of foam, and only then did he pour water on himself. He used a thin washcloth hanging on a nearby hook for drying.

"Yes," I finally answered.

"What did the doctor say?" he asked, turning toward me.

He is like a black diamond, I thought.

She said, I love you. "She said he must lose weight and watch what he eats. Nothing fattening. That he should rest at first and then start exercising. Walking would be best."

I watched Rajinder hang his shirt by the collar tips on the clothesline, and suddenly felt sad at the rigorous attention to detail necessary to preserve love. Perhaps love is different in other countries, I thought, where the climate is cooler, where a woman can say her husband's name, where the power does not go out every day, where not every clerk demands a bribe. That must be a different type of love, I thought, where one can be careless.

"It will rain tonight," he said, looking at the sky.

The eucalyptus trees shook their heads side to side. "The rain always makes me feel as if I am waiting for someone," I said, and then regretted saying it, for Rajinder was not paying attention, and perhaps it could have been said better. "Why don't you sit on the balcony, and I will make sherbet to drink?"

He took a chair and the newspaper with him. The fridge water was warm, and I felt sad again at the need for constant vigilance. I made the drink and gave him his glass. I placed mine on the floor and went to get a chair. A fruit seller passed by, calling out in a reedy voice, "Sweet, sweet mangoes. Sweeter than first love." On the roof directly across, a boy seven or eight years old was trying to fly a large purple kite. I sat down beside Rajinder and waited for him to look up so that I could interrupt his reading. When Rajinder looked away from the paper to take a sip of sherbet, I asked, "Did you fly kites?"

"A little," he answered, looking at the boy. "Ashok bought some with the money he earned, and he would let me fly them sometimes." The fact that his father had died when he was young made me hopeful, for I thought that one must suffer and be lonely before one can love.

"Do you like Ashok?"

"He is my brother," he answered, shrugging and looking at the newspaper. He took a sip of the sherbet. I felt hurt, as if he had reprimanded me.

I waited until seven for the power to return; then I gave up and started to prepare dinner in the dark. I sat beside Rajinder until then. I felt happy and excited and frightened being beside him. We spoke about Asha's going to America, though Rajinder did not want to talk about this. Rajinder had been the most educated member of his and my family and resented the idea that Asha would soon assume that position.

As I cooked in the kitchen, Rajinder sat on the balcony and listened to the radio. "This is Akashwani," the announcer said, and then music like horses racing played whenever a new program was about to start. It was very hot in the kitchen, and every now and then I stepped onto the roof to look at the curve of Rajinder's neck and confirm that the tenderness was still there.

We ate in the living room. Rajinder chewed slowly and was mostly silent. Once he complimented me on my cooking. "What are you thinking?" I asked. He appeared not to have heard. Tell me! Tell me! Tell me! I thought, and was shocked by the urgency I felt.

A candle on the television made pillars of shadows rise and collapse on the walls. I searched for something to start a conversation with. "Pitaji began crying when I left."

"You could have stayed a few more days," he said.

"I did not want to." I thought of adding, "I missed you," but that would have been a lie, and I would have felt embarrassed saying it, when he had not missed me.

Rajinder mixed black pepper with his yogurt. "Did you tell him you would visit soon?"

"No. I think he was crying because he was lonely."

"He should have more courage." Rajinder did not like Pitaji, thought him weak-willed, although Rajinder had never told me that. He knew Pitaji drank, but Rajinder never referred to this, for which I was grateful. "He is old and must remember that shadows creep into one's heart at his age." The shutter of a bedroom window began slamming, and I got up to latch it shut.

I washed the dishes while Rajinder bathed. When he came out, dressed in his white kurta pajamas, with his hair slicked back, I was standing near the railing at the roof's edge, looking out beyond the darkness of our neighborhood at a distant ribbon of light. I was tired from the nervousness I had been feeling all evening. Rajinder came up behind me and asked, "Won't you bathe?" I suddenly doubted my ability to guard my love. Bathe so we can have sex. His words were too deliberately full of the unsaid, and so felt vulgar. I wondered if I had the courage to say no and realized I didn't. What kind of love can we have? I thought.

I said, "In a little while. Comedy hour is about to start." We sat down on our chairs with the radio between us and listened to Maurya's whiny voice. This week he had gotten involved with criminals who wanted to go to jail to collect the reward on themselves. The canned laughter gusted from several flats. When the music of the racing horses marked the close of the show, I felt hopeful again, and thought Rajinder looked very handsome in his kurta pajamas.

I bathed carefully, pouring mug after mug of cold water over myself until my fingertips were wrinkled and my nipples erect. The candlelight made the bathroom orange and my skin copper. I washed my pubis carefully to make sure no smell remained from urinating. Rubbing myself dry, I became aroused. I wore the red sari again, with a new blouse, and no bra, so that my nipples would show.

I came and stood beside Rajinder, my arm brushing against his kurta sleeve. Every now and then a raindrop fell, and I wondered if I were imagining it. On balconies and roofs all around us I could see the dim figures of men, women, and children waiting for the first rain. "You look pretty," he said. Somewhere Lata Mangeshkar sang with a static-induced huskiness. The street was silent. Even the children were hushed. As the wind picked up, Rajinder said, "Let's close the windows."

The wind coursed along the floor, upsetting newspapers and climbing the walls to swing on curtains. A candle stood on the refrigerator. As I leaned over to pull a window shut, Rajinder pressed against me and cupped my right breast. I felt a shock of desire pass through me. As I walked around the rooms shutting windows, he touched my buttocks, pubis, stomach.

When the last window was closed, I waited for a moment before turning around, because I knew he wanted me to turn around quickly. He pulled me close, with his hands on my buttocks. I took his tongue in my mouth. We kissed like this for a long time.

The rain began falling, and we heard a roar from the people on the roofs nearby. "The clothes," Rajinder said, and pulled away.

We ran out. We could barely see each other. Lightning bursts would illuminate an eye, an arm, some teeth, and then darkness would come again. We jerked the clothes off and let the pins fall to the ground. We deliberately brushed roughly against each other. The raindrops were like thorns, and we began laughing. Rajinder's shirt had wrapped itself around and around the clothesline. Wiping his face, he knocked his glasses off. As I saw him crouch and fumble around helplessly for them, I felt such tenderness that I knew I would never love him as much as I did at that moment. "The wind in the trees," I cried out, "it sounds like the sea."

We slowly wandered back inside, kissing all the while. He entered me like a sigh. He suckled on me and moved back and forth and side to side, and I felt myself growing warm and loose. He sucked on my nipples and held my waist with both hands. We made love gently at first, but as we both neared climax, Rajinder began stabbing me with his penis and I came in waves so strong that I felt myself vanishing. When Rajinder sank on top of me, I kept saying, "I love you. I love you."

"I love you too," he answered. Outside, the rain came in sheets and the thunder was like explosions in caverns.

The candle had gone out while we made love, and Rajinder got up to light it. He drank some water and then lay down beside me. I wanted some water too, but did not want to say anything that would make him feel bad about his thoughtlessness. "I'll be getting promoted soon. Minaji loves me," Rajinder said. I rolled onto my side to look at him. He had his arms folded across his chest. "Yesterday he said, 'Come, Rajinderji, let us go write your confidential report.'" I put my hand on his stomach, and Rajinder said, "Don't," and pushed it away. "I said, 'Oh, I don't know whether that would be good, sir.'" He laughed and patted me on the back. "What a nincompoop. If it weren't for the quotas, he would never be manager." Rajinder chuckled. "I'll be the youngest bank manager in Delhi." I felt cold and tugged a sheet over our legs. "In college I had a schedule for where I wanted to be by the time I was thirty. By twenty-two I became an officer; soon I'll be a manager. I wanted a car, and we'll have that in a year. I wanted a wife, and I have that."

"You are so smart."

"Some people in college were smarter. But I knew exactly what I wanted. A life is like a house. One has to plan carefully where all the furniture will go."

"Did you plan me as your wife?" I asked, smiling.

"No. I had wanted at least an M.A., and someone who worked, but Mummy didn't approve of a daughter-in-law who worked. I was willing to change my requirements. Because I believe in moderation, I was successful. Everything in its place. And pay for everything. Other people got caught up in love and friendship. I've always felt that these things only became a big deal because of the movies."

"What do you mean? You love me and your mother, don't you?"

"There are so many people in the world that it is hard not to think that there are others you could love more."

Seeing the shock on my face, he quickly added, "Of course I love you. I just try not to be too emotional about it."

The candle's shadows on the wall were like the wavery bands formed by light reflected off water. "We might even be able to get a foreign car."

The second time he took me that night, it was from behind. He pressed down heavily on my back and grabbed my breasts.

I woke at four or five. The rain scratched against the windows and a light like blue milk shone along the edges of the door. I was cold and tried to wrap myself in the sheet, but it was not large enough.

A LIFE OF ADVENTURE AND DELIGHT

The side door of the police van slid open, rattling, and he was shoved inside. There were seven or eight men already sitting on the floor in the dark, their wrists handcuffed behind them. Nobody said anything. The van started with a jerk, then picked up speed. His legs were stretched out in front of him, and he tried to use his cuffed hands to balance himself, but the plastic cuffs tightened, and he and the other men went rolling across the floor like loose bottles.

This was the first time that Gautama had been arrested. Before calling the prostitute, he had Googled the number in the ad to make sure that it wasn't being used by the police. In the van, he remembered how, as he was being hurried down the stairs of his building, one of the apartment doors was slightly ajar, a man in an undershirt staring at him as he was led past.

Gautama was twenty-four, tall, slender, with large brown eyes and longish hair that framed his face. He was a Ph.D. student in chemistry at New York University. He had arrived in America a year earlier, and, like many foreign students in America who are living away from home for the first time, he had immediately begun loitering on Craigslist and Backpage.

The arrested men stood in a cell on one side of a brightly lit room. It was a little after midnight. A short, stocky policewoman was taking mug shots. When she was done, she came over and, looking bored, her hands on her hips, said, "You know, when you have sex with a prostitute you might as well be having sex with every guy she's slept with."

A bearded Hasidic man sidled up to the front of the cell. "I was just e-mailing the girl," he said. "I only offered money to help." He had a high cracking voice, and his eyes were very wide. He spoke so sincerely that he seemed to believe himself. A Latino guy in a blue mechanic's uniform was crouched in a corner of the cell, speaking tenderly through the bars to an underage prostitute who was seated on a folding chair, her slender wrist handcuffed to a bar. Until he began talking to the girl, the Latino had said only one thing, while being shoved into the van: "Shit, it's my birthday."

Around two in the morning, the men, all chained together, were led shuffling down the precinct steps. Gautama was near the end of the chain. The cold night air felt alien. He saw cars go by, their wheels hissing, and wanted to hide his face in his shoulder. The men ahead of him began climbing into the back of a white van. Gautama waited his turn, and as he did he felt that he and the other men had entered some strange narrow world—there was a world that was spacious and normal, where people drove home at night, and, next to it, off to the side, was another world that was so constricted that living in it was like walking between two pressed together walls.

In Central Booking, the men were led one by one into separate cells. The cells had bunk beds and steel toilets. In Gautama's cell, the wall beside the toilet bore long fingerlike streaks of shit. He lay down on the lower bunk. He was wearing a gray sweatshirt. He hugged himself and pulled his knees to his stomach.

Gautama was from Gwalior, a small city in Madhya Pradesh, one of those wretched places where the streets are narrow and crowded and where shopkeepers in the central market sell illegal postcards of suttees sitting on bonfires. When a merchant sold one to you, he'd touch the card to his forehead as if he wanted a last blessing before letting the goddess leave.

Gautama was an ordinary middle-class boy. He knew he would have to get married one day, and he hoped to have as much sex as possible before then, but he also believed that any Indian girl who had sex before marriage had something wrong with her, was in some way depraved and foul and also unintelligent. He wished he could have sex with Sunny Leone.

Gautama rolled over to face the cinder-block wall. From down the hall came the voice of a young man who had been in the holding cell with him. The young man had tried to start up conversations by asking the other men about their jobs. "I have cigarettes," he now called to whoever might be listening. "You OK," someone answered in fake solidarity.

Gautama's favorite thing about hiring prostitutes was negotiating the price. This was because actually having sex with a prostitute seemed so immoral that it was hard to enjoy it. As soon as he'd called a prostitute and left a message with a made-up name, he'd start to feel scared of what he'd set in motion, and a part of him would not want the woman to call back. If she did, he'd get excited. His mouth would go dry. He'd ask whether the hundred and fifty roses she asked for in her ad could be reduced. Often the woman hung up. Periodically, he and the prostitute would reach an agreement and set a time for her to come over. Most often then, in a panic, he would hurry out of the apartment. He lived in the Bronx, next to a bodega near the Grand Concourse. He would rush to put some distance between him and his building and then walk for hours, his heart racing. Whenever people glanced at him, he'd feel as if they might grab him and beat him.

Occasionally, Gautama stayed in his apartment and waited for the woman to arrive. His building was a walk-up, and he lived on the fourth floor, in a studio with a single large window, which was divided by metal brackets into many small panes. When the prostitute got to his apartment, she'd be out of breath and look irritated at having had to climb the stairs. He would invite her in and then tell her that she didn't look like the photos she'd texted and ask her to reduce her price again. As he did this, he was hoping that the woman would just demand cab fare and leave. Usually, she shouted at him. Sometimes, cursing him, she reduced the price by ten or fifteen dollars. The actual sex after all this was almost always wretched: Gautama wearing double condoms, and the woman beneath him looking angry, telling him, "Don't touch the breasts."

As he lay on his side in the cell, a thought came to him: he should just get married. Most of his cousins who were his age were married already. He felt that if he were married he wouldn't hire prostitutes, he wouldn't be ridiculous, he wouldn't do things like call a hooker and ask if the "afternoon delight" rate still applied, even though it was evening.

AT ELEVEN THE NEXT morning, Gautama was released.

For two days, he went to a park and picked up litter while wearing an orange vest. Kids went whizzing by him on bicycles, calling, "What you did, punk?" When he didn't respond, one of them, emboldened, stopped a few feet from him and shouted, "I'll make you my bitch!" It seemed to him that this was the world that his actions had brought him into. He picked up garbage and imagined being married, being a father, having a son. He imagined working hard and earning money to take care of his family. Imagining this, he felt comforted, as if he were already living that life.

Nirmala was a little over five feet tall. She had a round face and a round body and shiny black hair. She liked to gossip and laugh, especially about politicians. She, too, was from a small city, from a family of doctors. She had not been able to get into medical school, so she was getting a Ph.D. in biology. Nirmala was popular among the foreign graduate students. Partly this was because she was cheerful. Partly, also, it was because she was kind. She always remembered people's birthdays and tried to organize a cake or a dinner or at least a card. When somebody was sick, she visited and brought food. Gautama had spoken to Nirmala only a few times. Since other people respected her, he assumed she was admirable.

Nirmala worked at the circulation desk in the big atrium at Bobst Library. Gautama began drifting among the shelves of reference books to look at her. Normally, she took her lunch break at twelve thirty. One day, he walked up to the circulation desk. He felt self-conscious about his face, about his long body, about the fact that his breath might smell of coffee. "Do you want to have lunch?" he asked, and giggled.

"With you?"

"Yes."

The graduate students from India, even when they didn't know each other well, treated one another with the politeness of people who live in the same lane.

Gautama and Nirmala went to a seminar room to eat. There was a conference table, a whiteboard, a projector on a rolling table. They had brought their lunches in plastic grocery-store bags, and when they sat down, she asked what kind of water his city had. "Hard water," he said, and she told him that she still found it amazing that in America one could drink from the tap.

They removed the aluminum foil their rotis were rolled up in. The crinkling of the foil sounded loud to Gautama. At first, they ate in silence, like people traveling together on a bus. Gautama had been imagining what kind of marriage he wanted, and he felt he needed to be as honest as possible in order to have the sort of relationship he was envisioning. He told Nirmala the thing that felt most precious to him.

"My sister has epilepsy."

Gautama's parents had not told his sister, his only sibling, what condition she had. They had told him instead, because he was a boy. His sister was four years older than he was, and his relationship with her had always involved his feeling that he'd had good luck while she'd had bad. He was haunted by the image of his sister swallowing pills whose purpose she didn't understand, standing beside the kitchen sink, taking one pill from their mother's outstretched palm and then a second and then opening her mouth to show their mother that it was empty.

In India, public knowledge of his sister's epilepsy would have marked the whole family as defective. Telling someone about her for the first time, Gautama felt careless, immature, selfish. "When we began looking for a boy for her, my parents had to tell whoever was considering her about the epilepsy," he said. Several of the families his parents negotiated with declined to pursue a marriage. One finally agreed to it after his parents promised a house in the city, a farm, and a foreign car. After the dowry had been agreed upon, the groom's grandfather, feeling that he had not been adequately consulted, forbade the marriage.

Gautama was seventeen then. He went with his father to the electronics shop that the groom's family owned. They stood in the parking lot outside the shop, surrounded by scooters. The sun was hot, and the diesel in the air hurt Gautama's eyes and throat.

His father pleaded with the grandfather, who was wearing a white kurta pajama. "What is the matter?" his father said, touching the old man's elbow. "She is a good girl. We have ordered the food for the engagement."

"You tried to be smart, didn't you?" the old man scolded. "Trying to hide your shame with such a large dowry."

Because of her epilepsy, his sister, who had a bachelor's degree, was now married to a laborer who had not finished high school. The man lived in Saudi Arabia doing construction work, and his parents treated Gautama's sister as a servant.

As Nirmala listened, she looked concerned. After he'd finished speaking, she was silent for a while. Softly, she said, "When your sister's children are ready for education, you can pay for it." She said this because she knew that sometimes the only relief possible is the thought that one day we'll be able to help in some small way. But Gautama had so much adrenaline in him that he had a hard time understanding what she was saying. She seemed to be talking about something other than what he had just told her.

Several hours later, sitting in an office chair, looking at a computer screen, in a very cold lab, he began to feel an unclenching. Having told somebody about his sister made the world feel bigger, as if there were more space around him. Simultaneously, the way fresh air can cause a cut to sting, a new sense of horror arrived at the image of his mother standing by his sister, making her swallow pills whose mysteriousness frightened her, and then saying "Open" until his sister opened her empty mouth.

NIRMALA AND GAUTAMA began having lunch together every day. After a few days, Gautama stopped being nervous about asking her to join him.

They ate in seminar rooms that had glass walls and white-boards. When they finished eating, they'd wipe down the table with wet paper towels. Then they'd take the plastic bags they'd brought their lunches in into the hallway and put them in the trash cans there, so that the odor would disperse. They did this because they felt self-conscious about the stereotype of how Indians smell.

Nirmala was flattered by Gautama's attention. She saw herself as fat, lumbering. Once, a friend, a white girl who also worked at the circulation desk, gestured with her head toward Gautama as he walked over to them. "Your shadow has arrived," she said. Nirmala knew that her friend was teasing, but having a shadow pleased her. She thought more often about Gautama, and as she thought more often about him he began to gain in importance for her.

After his arrest, Gautama had stopped going onto Backpage. Once he started having lunch with Nirmala, he also stopped looking at pornography. He did this because he wanted there to be no shame in his relationship with her.

As the days went by and they continued having lunch, he told her stories and found himself relieved of old anxieties.

His family ran a nuts-and-dried-fruit business, and he told her how, when he was thirteen or fourteen, he had conspired with a family employee to steal money from one of the shops his family owned. The man had then blackmailed him. After he told Nirmala this, the guilt of having stolen from his family, the sense of self-disgust for being so weak that he could be blackmailed, dissipated almost immediately. It vanished so quickly that it was like waking from a nightmare and within minutes not being able to recall what had happened in the dream.

One night, a month after they started having lunch, they went out to dinner. An Indian restaurant had opened on crowded Macdougal Street, and Gautama had read in a magazine that the restaurant, for its opening weeks, while it worked out its menu, was allowing guests to pay whatever they thought was fair. Gautama's plan was to pay nothing. It didn't occur to him that Nirmala would mind this.

The restaurant was in a basement. They went down some steps and entered a room with a dozen or so tables with white tablecloths. Only a few of the tables were occupied. Eight young Indians, probably undergraduates, were seated around the largest table, in the middle of the room, and the manager, an Indian man with a mustache, went over to them frequently to see how they were liking the meal. He didn't go as often to the tables with white customers. Gautama understood that the manager was suspicious that the Indians would try to get away with paying nothing. He saw this and felt in his stomach that he, too, would not have entered a restaurant with no intention of paying if it were owned by white people.

The manager came over to Gautama and Nirmala. He explained the pricing: "What would food like this cost in another restaurant? That is one way to think of it." He spoke in the stretched vowels of an Indian trying to sound American. He left them to look at the menu.

Nirmala watched him go. "Are you planning not to pay?" she asked.

"I'll pay something," Gautama murmured. He stared down at the menu, which was a single page with a list of items on the left side and nothing on the right.

"Shrimp is expensive," Nirmala said. "Fish is expensive. We can't steal from these people."

The fact that she wanted to pay when she didn't have to surprised him. A part of him couldn't believe it. He felt that she was showing off.

"I didn't bring my purse. You should have told me to bring my wallet," she said.

Hearing her frustration, he had the sense that he did not know her, that he had been revealing himself to someone who might have been thinking bad things about him.

The manager came back with a waiter. He explained again that they should bear in mind what the food might cost in another restaurant.

Nirmala ordered without looking up. She asked for the lentils, which would probably have been the cheapest item on the menu. "I'll have the turmeric fish," Gautama said, "and the seafood biryani." He ordered two entrées because, despite the fear of embarrassment, he couldn't pass up something free.

"It is a lot of food," the manager said. At his American-sounding accent, Gautama felt even more judged. He kept looking down. The manager stood there for a moment and then left.

Gautama and Nirmala sat in silence. The food came. They began eating.

"This isn't very good," Gautama said.

"I don't want to talk."

He continued eating. He wondered what he should pay.

The meal ended. The manager came to their table and asked how they had enjoyed the food.

"It was very good," Nirmala said. "We'll come back."

He put down a printout of all the items they had ordered. Gautama placed seventy dollars on top of it. This was all the money he had.

Outside, it was a cold February night. There were people waiting in lines to get into restaurants. Some of them were arm in arm. One couple walked in circles, laughing at how cold it was. As Gautama and Nirmala walked down the crowded sidewalk, Nirmala bumped into him. "Sorry," Gautama said, not looking at her. After a few steps, she bumped into him again. He glanced at her.

"It's over," she said, and laughed.

Gautama felt relieved that he had not embarrassed himself before Nirmala.

AS HE GOT TO KNOW HER better, Nirmala began to seem more complicated to him. She told him that her father's younger brother had "bothered" her. She didn't say what he had done to bother her, but she said that, when her uncle was living with her family, she had begun pulling out her hair. "I get white hair where I used to pull it out," she said.

The fact that this had happened to her made Gautama see her as being like any other person, someone with her own past, someone who needed love, who was scared and embarrassed, who had pulled out her own hair and was convinced that it turned white because of this.

The two started going on walks in the evening in the West Village, near Nirmala's dorm. One day, they held hands for the first time. It was mid-March. The air was cold and heavy with moisture. They were walking past a pizza parlor, and Nirmala put her hand in his. The first thing Gautama noticed was the calluses on her palms. But as soon as he had closed his hand around hers, he had the feeling that he would never need anything else. All the other things he worried about—his research, what job he would get, what might happen to his family in India—none of this mattered, because this thing was OK.

He looked on YouTube for guidance on kissing. He watched a video in which an old white-haired couple kissed and then told each other what they had liked about the kiss.

French kissing seemed disrespectful. Kissing with closed lips had the bravery of kissing—a declaration of not caring what society thought—but was also not vulgar.

Every new thing that he and Nirmala did, such as standing on a street corner, each with a hand in the other's back pocket, gave him a sense of freedom. They began lying together on her bed in her dorm room, kissing until he stopped being able to think. He would move her hand to his crotch, and she would move it away.

Gautama began looking at pornography again. He felt that if he did not ejaculate he would go mad. The first time he did this, sitting at his small wooden desk in his apartment, his laptop open before him, he immediately wondered why he had worried so much about doing it.

He began to find Nirmala incredibly beautiful. Her ears, small with little diamond studs, appeared both modest and intelligent. When she spoke, her soft insistent voice resounded as if it were inside his own chest.

In early June, they decided to have sex. They removed their clothes and stood in Nirmala's dorm room.

"Don't look at me," she said, holding her hands over her stomach.

He knelt down and kissed her belly.

"Does it smell bad?" she asked.

"No. Why?"

"I don't know."

In the days afterward, in the happiness of someone having chosen to have sex with him, he felt that he was growing more real, more substantial. Before, he had been only thoughts and emotions, and now he was becoming solid.

He found himself constantly thinking about Nirmala, how he teased her about her nervousness about her weight: "You are so small that you get lost in the bed." He pictured some of the things they had done, him half sitting, with her on top of him, telling her that she was not heavy, that she was like a little girl. To be able to be kind to someone you loved seemed a fortunate thing.

Until then, they had kept their involvement a secret. Once, at a Holi party, a large, dark-skinned woman from Hyderabad had begun praising Nirmala in front of Gautama, as if inviting him to join in. Gautama had immediately become suspicious that the woman might be a gossip, that if he were to say what he felt the woman would then tell others and the information might somehow make its way to India, where it could be used to embarrass Nirmala's family.

But now Nirmala began introducing him to people as her boyfriend. This felt dangerous to Gautama, as if they were taking on a problem they could have avoided. He wondered whether Nirmala was doing this so that he could not back out. He decided that he did not want to think such a thing about her, that she was simply declaring her love to the world.

He and Nirmala began to be treated as a couple. People would ask him what hours she was working. Once, a woman came to him and wanted to know if Nirmala's aunt in New Jersey was going to be visiting India soon, because she wanted to send a blood-pressure cuff to a relative. There was a strain to being known as a couple. One man advised him to propose in the morning; that way he and Nirmala would have the whole day to enjoy being engaged. At a party, he talked to a woman who was a new Ph.D. student, and one of Nirmala's friends stood nearby glaring angrily at him.

Because Nirmala's parents were bound to learn about him, it seemed important to tell his parents first, so that they might reach out to hers and keep them from feeling shame.

Gautama sat cross-legged on his futon bed and Skyped with his mother. She started crying. She wiped her eyes with a fold of her sari while his father's legs paced behind her. They were contemplating the dowry they could have negotiated, Gautama assumed, the elation there would have been in finding a match for a son who was educated in America. "I blame you, not her," his mother said, and from this he understood that all was not lost. His father shouted, "I blame her, too!"

Afterward, Gautama went to the refrigerator and stood by it drinking milk to ease his stomach.

In the next few days, he got calls from his sister, from his favorite cousin, from an uncle whom everybody in the family was scared of because he was a small-time politician and gangster. The tension of this was constant, and Gautama felt that he could not talk about it with Nirmala, because he had had sex with her, and so she had tied her fate to his.

Weeks went by, and then months. He periodically told his mother that she should talk to Nirmala, that Nirmala was a good girl. "When I have to drink that poison, I will," she said.

Some things about Nirmala began to irritate him. If they went to a movie, she would take the tickets from his hand after he had purchased them. When they went to buy groceries, she would check that all the items on their list were in the cart, even though he had already crossed them out on the scrap of paper they were written on. To Gautama, this behavior seemed to come from Nirmala's belief that if she were not in charge things would go wrong. Sometimes he wondered what he had started.

What bothered him most about Nirmala was that, if he was incorrect about something, she would point it out immediately. If he did the same to her, she became sullen. Once, he told her that the argument she was making about genetics was probably not correct. When he explained why he'd said this, she became angry and asked why he was in such a bad mood.

September came, and the university became busy again. The weather was still warm, and every afternoon two young women on Rollerblades performed in Washington Square Park. They wore white shorts and skated around the arch while playing trumpets. Gautama liked looking at these women so much that he would try always to be in Washington Square when they were there.

ONE EVENING, ALMOST A YEAR after he was arrested, he sat at his desk and opened his laptop and went to Backpage. The screen filled with ads: lines of text, some words in bold, others capitalized, phone numbers written out as words. He felt as if he were floating, as if it were someone else's finger clicking on an ad. A new screen opened: more text with images below, a Hispanic girl in a bikini, her face hidden by a flash, the picture taken in a bathroom mirror. Gautama recognized the photo from other ads he'd seen, and he suddenly became exhausted at the memory of calling prostitutes and then running away from his apartment. He shut down the computer.

A few days later, he came home and opened his laptop before he'd finished undressing. He sat on the edge of his futon and browsed through Backpage. He had his jeans at his ankles, and he remained that way for an hour.

The prostitute who walked into his apartment later that night was nineteen or twenty and black. She had white plastic beads in her hair. It was dark outside, and his studio's wide window, divided into panes, was like a bank of TV screens in which the girl hung bright and tilted.

The girl stood at the center of the room, and Gautama's heart pounded. Before she arrived, he had planned to tell her that she did not look like her photo and give her cab fare home. But she was much more beautiful than her photo, and he thought that the luck of getting someone so lovely might not occur again, and, since he would eventually end up having sex with a prostitute anyway, it was best not to waste this opportunity.

The girl was wearing a gray dress with thin blue horizontal stripes. Gautama handed her the money. He stepped away from her and again was amazed by her beauty.

"You're pretty," he said.

"Thank you."

"Could you take off all your clothes?"

She pulled her dress over her head. She was slender with big breasts. She looked as if she had been Photoshopped. Folding the dress, she put it on his desk, which stood near the head of the bed. She came back to the center of the room.

"May I hold your breasts while you jump?"

The girl laughed. "Sure."

She was smiling as he put his hands on her breasts. She started jumping. Her hair flew up, and the beads clicked. Her feet made soft thuds when she landed.

His hands on her breasts, Gautama became happier and happier. He knew that tomorrow he would feel guilt and shame, but he did not care. The girl jumped, and he had the sense that nobody else anywhere could be leading a life of such adventure and delight.

A HEART IS SUCH A HEAVY THING

Arun Kumar had just turned twenty-four when he decided that he would marry the chubby, round-faced girl he had never met. Four months ago, he had gotten his first job, as a bookkeeper for Toyota Tonics. With his new employment, and its endless supply of tonic, he had taken to drinking many bottles of the sugary stuff every day. Arun, finally a man, a man with a job, decided that it was time he gained some weight. And, finally a man, a man with a job, Arun agreed to his father's pleas to consider marriage. And so, late one evening, the word went around that Arun was looking for a wife, and in no time he and his family were playing host to a procession of fathers, almost all of them strangers, who appeared, one after another, bearing black-and-white photographs of their daughters in various poses and with varying degrees of ugliness. This went on for three months. And then one day, Vinod Mishra, the father of Namrita, appeared. Namrita, Arun could see, was not ugly, just pudgy, and she had, as well, a sizable dowry, and Arun threw up his hands and said, "Why not? I get along with everyone. So why not her?"

Arun Kumar was still twenty-four, but he was now a twenty-four-year-old with a job and a fiancée. (The wedding would be next month.) And, finally, he was starting to gain some weight. What he now needed was a better job—that was just the thing before he got married—and his father, Prasad Kumar, had just the solution: he would make his son a teacher.

PRASAD KUMAR WANTED his son to meet Mr. Gupta, Prasad Kumar's supervisor and the head of the physical education department at the Delhi municipality where they both worked. Mr. Gupta was a man of influence, and had promised that he might be able to do something for Prasad Kumar's son. There was to be a wedding reception at Mr. Gupta's home for his son, Narayan.

Strings of small blue and red lightbulbs hung three stories down the front of the Gupta house. Mr. Gupta stood at the gates of the courtyard greeting guests. Behind him waiters in red turbans, white jackets, and white pants moved among the visitors. Electric fans, five feet tall, stood every few steps along the courtyard's walls. Arun and his father were there to offer their congratulations. "You want to be a teacher, Arun?" Mr. Gupta asked.

The answer was so obvious that Arun wondered whether he was being teased. Mr. Gupta had already made his promise. The only reason Prasad Kumar had brought Arun to the party was to make Mr. Gupta feel obligated to keep his word.

"Yes," Arun said.

"Mr. Gupta can help," Prasad Kumar said.

"I can try," Mr. Gupta said modestly.

"If you knew all the people Mr. Gupta knew you would go mad," Prasad Kumar said. Arun's father could flatter people so extravagantly that he stopped making sense.

"Your father compliments me five times a day, like a Muslim saying his prayers," Mr. Gupta said.

"Most Muslims are far from Mecca, while I sit just down the hall from you," Prasad Kumar replied.

Mr. Gupta laughed. "See how far shamelessness will take you."

A couple arrived behind them. The man wore a kurta pajama, and the woman had on a dress. A cosmopolitan mixture, Arun thought.

Prasad Kumar raised his voice to make sure they heard: "All Mr. Gupta has to do is look at someone and the person gets a job, a wife, a government flat." He nodded at his own words.

"Go in, Mr. Kumar," Mr. Gupta said, gesturing.

Prasad Kumar took a folded envelope with a hundred and one rupees inside and gave it to Mr. Gupta. "For your son's new life," he said, and shook Mr. Gupta's hand one more time.

As they stepped into the courtyard, Prasad Kumar, who was fat and bald except for a ridge of hair on either side of his scalp, slipped an arm around Arun's waist. "That is how you speak to powerful people, Fatso," he said. "They know you're exaggerating, but they like it, and you keep your pride because you also know you're exaggerating."

The rich, his father was always saying, may be better or smarter, but there are still ways to make them do what you want.

Near the courtyard they met Mrs. Chauduri, the municipality's senior junior physical education officer. She was short—very, very short—but, in fact, just tall enough, technically, not to be a dwarf.

"Auntiji, how is your health?" Arun asked.

"It is as God wills," Mrs. Chauduri sighed. Two years earlier, she had undergone a double mastectomy.

"God is testing you," Arun said. The phrase pleased him, and he could see that Mrs. Chauduri was pleased to have her troubles made purposeful and dramatic.

"And you will pass," his father added.

A waiter edged by, and Prasad Kumar exclaimed, "Tonight, I will drink only whiskey!"

Other physical education officers began gathering around them. They, like Arun and his father, wore only shirts and pants. Nearly all the other men in the courtyard wore suits.

At some point, Prasad Kumar decided to declare the closeness of his relationship with Mr. Gupta by getting drunk. "We should get crazy," he said. Prasad Kumar promptly poured an entire glass of whiskey down his throat.

Arun and Mrs. Chauduri exchanged glances.

"You are a good boy," Mrs. Chauduri whispered to Arun, as

if to offer comfort. "I am going to tell Mr. Gupta that you are a good boy." Mrs. Chauduri then slipped into the crowd and disappeared.

Of the three rooms abutting the courtyard, only the central one had its doors open. The food was in there, and the room was so packed that plates were being passed back out over people's heads. They were shouting and laughing in the struggle. A woman holding a boy's hand stood near the doorway saying, "Let us through." No one did. Arun stood a few feet from the woman. He was finding the undisguised greed unsettling.

A waiter passed, and Arun ordered a drink. "Can you fill the whole glass?" he asked. He had drunk perhaps five times in his life, and hated alcohol, but because it was free he felt obliged to consume as much as possible.

"All you have to do is ask, sir," the waiter said, and Arun immediately knew the man would want a tip.

Nearby, he saw a fat woman wearing a sleeveless maroon blouse and gold bangles on both arms. She was eating from a plate piled high with cubes of cheese. Since this was the hottest time of the year, when the cows produced very little milk, cheese was very expensive. It occurred to Arun that this cheese must have been scattered carefully throughout the trays of food hidden in the press of bodies, and the fat woman must have gathered it with care. The way she was hoarding this delicacy made Arun think of his father flattering Mr. Gupta for favors: they were both petty, desperate acts of greed. Such desperation was everywhere. The fat woman noticed his stare and turned her face to the wall.

The whiskey came, a full glass. The waiter stood beside him

for a minute and in a low voice repeated, "Reward, sir, reward." Arun avoided his eyes.

The first sip of the bitter stuff made him gag. He continued drinking, though, standing in a corner near a fan, with the whiskey hidden between his hands.

"Happy?" his father boomed from somewhere in the courtyard. He often greeted people this way when he was cheerfully drunk. Arun could not see him. "Happy?" came the voice again.

There was a stir in the crowd, and Arun spotted his father standing close to an extremely thin man. Alcohol had turned his father's face red, making him look angry. As a child, Arun used to be so afraid when his father came home drunk that the only way he could sleep was wedged against a wall under his cot. He felt that fear now, but instead of paralyzing him it made him angry, even eager to fight. Arun was pleased by the anger.

The man said something, and Prasad Kumar shouted, "How happy?" The man responded, and Prasad Kumar, lifting his arms as if he were about to dance, began singing the words "Listen, love, listen." Prasad Kumar was a good singer, and even when he was drunk his voice had personality, a patient whimsy. The crowd shifted again. Seeing his father's talent, Arun's anger diminished.

A second room edging the courtyard was opened, and inside, sitting on red thrones, were the groom and the bride. The groom wore a blue suit, and the woman wore a red sari, a fold of which was pulled up to cover her face.

As Arun moved to join a queue that was forming to offer

the couple congratulations, he felt a hand on his arm. It was Mr. Gupta.

"Your father wants you," he said, and pinched Arun's sleeve to direct him through the crowd. From the tightness of Mr. Gupta's face, Arun knew what had happened: his father was already unmanageably drunk.

He found his father outside, on the side of the road, standing close to a short, dark-skinned businessman named Mr. Maurya. When Arun was a child and Mr. Maurya was struggling in his business, he used to visit their flat with bottles of rum and whiskey and spend the night on the roof wheedling his father for favors. Now Mr. Maurya was trying to get into his white Ambassador sedan.

"You weren't too busy to come see me when your only business was recycling the paper from schools!" Prasad Kumar was saying, so loudly that Arun could hear him from the courtyard gates. Arun crossed the road.

His father persisted. "You should let me do things for you."

"If I have work, I'll call you," Mr. Maurya said, looking Prasad Kumar in the eye. Arun stopped about ten feet from his father. Fright kept him from going any closer.

Mr. Maurya opened his car door and got in, but Prasad Kumar suddenly lurched forward, wedging himself in front of the door before Mr. Maurya could shut it. Ignoring him, Mr. Maurya slipped the key into the ignition and started the car. Prasad Kumar climbed into the sedan, shoving the smaller man aside. The engine whirred. For a long moment, Mr. Maurya and Prasad Kumar sat crushed together in the driver's seat. Then, suddenly, Prasad Kumar got out again. Mr. Maurya quickly repositioned himself behind the steering wheel and shut the car door. Prasad Kumar stood breathing heavily and looking at the ground. Arun was frozen in embarrassment, with the alcohol in him vanishing in a flare of fear. He stood there immobile, beside his father, as the sedan rolled away.

THE 100 BUS back to the Old Vegetable Market, where the Kumar family lived, was nearly empty. Prasad Kumar and his son sat in the back. They had not spoken during the wait at the stand and were silent now. Arun was thinking of his forthcoming wedding, how disappointing it would be for someone to be married to a man as confused and ridiculous as himself.

"Mr. Maurya has seen me drunk before," Prasad Kumar said at last. "He used to bring me bottles of Old Monk Rum." They passed the fenced fields of the police academy. The fields were empty and wide.

"What does Mr. Maurya care? I do anything he wants." A little later he began gasping as he prepared for tears. Arun's father usually cried after getting drunk.

Prasad Kumar put his hand on his son's thigh. The bus swung around a corner. The conductor, a young man, was watching them in the rearview mirror. Prasad Kumar continued now in a full flow of tears, "If Mrs. Chauduri would just retire, I would then become senior junior officer. She comes to the office only once a week." Arun stared out the window. He was unhappy. He sat still under his father's hand. Where had his anger gone—the anger he'd felt when he heard his father shouting "Happy?"

Prasad Kumar gave several long shaking sighs, as if in satisfaction. Then he said, "I wonder what Mrs. Chauduri's husband thinks of her not having breasts." By the time they had crossed Malka Ganj and Arun could see the Old Clock Tower, his father's sighs had almost ended. As they slowed for their stop, Prasad Kumar wiped his cheeks with both hands. "If I didn't drink," he said, "everything would be different for me." Prasad Kumar yawned and unbuttoned one of his cuffs. Then he started on the other one, as if he were already home and undressing.

ARUN WAS TO BE MARRIED in three days. This was the last time he would be allowed out of the flat until the wedding. (The wedding deposits were nonrefundable; he had to be kept from the evil eye.) "As a wedding present, I'm going to hang myself from the fan above your bed," said Suresh. Suresh was Arun's twelve-year-old brother. "You'll come into your room, turn on the light and the fan at the same time, and my body will start twisting."

"You don't weigh enough to choke by hanging," Arun said.

"I'll tie bricks to my feet."

"If you want to stop the wedding, remember to kill yourself before, not after, we are married." Now that the wedding was only a few days away, the family had begun making nervous jokes about how the marriage was a mistake.

It was night, and they were walking home through the Old Vegetable Market. The paths between the stalls were narrowing as their owners, in preparation for shutting down, threw rubbish out for the cows to eat. Only a few of the stalls still had their kerosene lamps lit, and at these the owners were stacking the plates of their scales. The air smelled of coriander and wet green things.

"Why don't you run away?" Suresh said. "I can give you twenty-three rupees." He had meant this to be a joke, but as this was all the money he had, the words came out with too much gravity. "Shoelaces cost ten," Arun said.

They stopped and bought several bananas, each just a little longer than an index finger. Arun, distracted by his thoughts, was talking less and less these days. The brothers had only two more nights of sleeping on side-by-side cots on the open roof. All the nights after that, Arun and his new wife would be hidden from view in the roof's only room, a small yellow one.

"I have to get strong for my wife," Arun said, shoving a whole banana into his mouth.

Suresh put two bananas into his mouth and, pretending they were tusks, began to swing his head.

They continued walking. Suresh said, "She probably stinks because she's fat."

"Don't say such a mean thing," Arun said.

Suresh felt chided.

They took a few more steps and Arun slipped an arm around Suresh's shoulders.

They left the stalls and proceeded along the high sidewalk that ran till Old Clock Tower Road met Malka Ganj Road at the police station. A few cots had been set out on the pavement, and there were men sitting on them and playing cards by candlelight. "Reasonable people cannot behave badly toward each other when both know that a marriage is for life," Arun said.

They had reached the mouth of the alley that led to their doorway. Suresh wanted to say something, but he did not know what. "Let's go drink some milk."

"I want to get home," Arun said. He paused, noticing how his silence was affecting Suresh, and added, "I'm not unhappy, I'm frightened." He pinched the back of his brother's neck. "Let's go sleep."

THE CEREMONY WENT ON all night in a tent in a field near the bride's house. When the prayers had been said, Arun's mother, Indira, hurried the bride along so that Arun's relatives could go home and rest. There were about thirty in all, and by seven a chartered bus had unloaded them in the Old Vegetable Market. By eight they were all squeezed into the Kumars' small flat, most of them (including three snoring children beneath the dining table) on the floor. Relatives were everywhere, all now deep in slumber. It was dark, and the only two people stirring were Namrita and her new mother-in-law.

Namrita was in the flat's entry hall, sitting on a corner of a thin mattress in the entry hall. The rest of the space had been taken up by members of two heavily breathing families. Namrita was expected to stay up in case friends and well-wishers came around to call on her.

Her mother-in-law was squatting underneath a counter, looking into the flour tin. Indira, all sinews and deeply wrinkled loose skin, was anxious about the amount of food she was going to have to cook for the relatives. The kitchen was so narrow that only one person could move between the counters. As she examined the flour, she thought that mostly their relatives were selfish and unreliable.

"Where is the shampoo, please?" Namrita asked. She was standing in the kitchen doorway with her sari pulled up to veil her face. She was plump enough that her stomach hung over the waist of her sari.

"We don't have shampoo," Indira said.

Namrita didn't move.

"Could someone get shampoo?" Namrita asked.

"Use soap," Indira said abruptly, and more loudly than she had intended.

Namrita left.

After marrying Prasad Kumar, Indira had moved into his family's home, where, disliking her without cause, his sisters had hidden the soap. She had remained silent on the matter, not wishing to appear a complainer. Now, in a similar situation, Namrita's question appeared so bold that Indira wondered whether something was wrong with the girl's mind. There had already been difficulties in getting the promised dowry. To be completely deceived into accepting a daughter-in-law who was crazy did not, under the circumstances, appear impossible. In fact, Indira knew of several marriages in which madness (and worse) was discovered after everything had been done, and the only solution had been divorce. A nephew of hers was still with a woman who was periodically possessed by ghosts. And the son of an acquaintance had married a heroin addict, whose habit was discovered only when syringes started clogging the toilet. A cousin had married a man who always wore socks, even when he was in the bath. Later, her cousin tugged off his socks while he was asleep and found leprous purple stumps.

Forty minutes later, Namrita returned.

"Can I do some yoga?" she asked. "Otherwise I might fall asleep."

Namrita's eccentricity was starting to make Indira genuinely afraid.

"Where?"

"On the roof, maybe?"

On the roof! She imagined her heavy daughter-in-law sitting up there before the world, trying to drag a leg behind her neck. She was now certain that Namrita was mad.

"Go back and sit," Indira hissed.

Indira washed her hands and then went to wake her husband. Prasad Kumar was asleep on the floor with his body halfway beneath a cot.

Indira nudged her husband awake.

"Come outside," she whispered.

They went onto the balcony, which looked down over a squatter colony made up of mud huts. It was so hot they were both sweating.

"This girl," Indira said, but her voice came out so shrill that she stopped. She climbed a short flight of steps to the roof. Her husband followed.

Arun was sleeping in the roof's small yellow room. "This girl is crazy," Indira said in a quieter voice. She told him about the shampoo and the yoga, glancing at Arun's room as she spoke.

"That's not so bad," Prasad Kumar said. "You're that crazy yourself?"

"Going to the open roof to do yoga? The day after your wedding?"

Prasad Kumar lifted a shoulder in a tired shrug. "You haven't slept," he said.

"I was seventeen when I married you and had better manners. Namrita is twenty-three."

"Her mother is crazy, too," said Prasad Kumar.

They heard steps coming up the stairs. It was Suresh. The latrine was near the balcony.

"Has there been a murder?" he asked.

"Your mother thinks Namrita is crazy."

Suresh smiled at the possibility of scandal. "Why?"

Indira explained.

"That is strange," he said, and a moment later added, "My question is, where is the dowry?"

Namrita's family had provided the dowry in the form of furniture instead of cash. They had done this without consulting anyone. But there was no space in the flat, and the furniture had been returned and a promise of cash extracted. Arun's family had expected the money at the wedding, but only a few thousand rupees had turned up.

"They give us a washer and we have water two hours a day?" Indira said. Arun's family had been persuaded to keep a large washing machine. It had been put in the yellow room on the roof. "Would sane people do that?"

"Oh, God," Prasad Kumar sighed. The possibility of no dowry suddenly seemed real.

"Return the girl," Indira said. She was feeling cheated.

"We could have got a motorcycle, a Honda, for Arun," Suresh said, needling his father. "But if you return her now, her parents will go to the police saying that we demanded money."

"How could I know they would be so cunning?" Prasad Kumar said in a heavy voice.

Suresh went to the room on the roof and knocked.

"Hello," Arun called from inside.

He was smiling when he opened the door, and Indira wondered if he had been awake, listening to them. The ceiling fan was spinning, and the floor was wet from the water Arun had poured out to evaporate and dull the heat. Arun went back to the bed and lay down. He was wearing only shorts, and his stomach spread out on either side of him. Everyone stepped inside and sat along the edge of the bed.

Indira told the yoga story once more. Telling it so often was beginning to take away its power for her.

"Couldn't she be crazy?" she asked.

"She's not like us," Arun said softly.

"Who gives a washing machine to someone in the Old Vegetable Market?" Prasad Kumar asked. The washer was in a corner, covered with a yellow sheet.

"What about the dowry?" Suresh asked.

"That money is gone," Arun said, and chuckled.

"What are you showing your teeth for?" Indira said.

"It's a good day. I've gotten married. That's why I'm laughing," Arun said. He grabbed his stomach and shook it.

"The boy's gone crazy for the girl," Prasad Kumar said, disgusted.

"See, 'crazy,'" Arun said, holding his stomach to be looked at.

"Quiet," Indira said. "All Delhi is sleeping downstairs."

Suresh lay down beside his brother and fell asleep almost immediately. Then Prasad Kumar crawled over them and put a pillow beneath his own head. Indira stood and watched and still felt that some wrong had been done her, but she did not know whom to blame.

"You can't sleep because of the pain that big smile causes?" Indira asked.

Arun giggled. He did not close his eyes, and Indira did not move. She had begun to feel tired.

There was a knock. It was Namrita. Arun covered his bare chest with a pillow. Namrita was holding a tray with five cups of tea and a saucer of sugar. She kept a fold of her sari over her face by clenching it between her teeth.

Namrita eyed the room. "What's under the sheet?" she asked.

"A washing machine," Suresh answered, staring at her.

"Why?"

"Your father gave it," Prasad Kumar said.

"You don't use it?"

"Two buckets of water a day would be more useful."

When Namrita realized the problem, she began laughing, and the fold of sari that had been covering her face slid onto her shoulders. "You can store clothes in it," she said. Arun began laughing, too. Namrita smiled at him, and Indira thought for the first time that what she had first seen as a sign of insanity might just be directness.

It made her think of her own marriage, how bravely and willfully she had entered it. She hadn't asked questions of anyone; she had wanted only to do what was expected of her—that, she believed, would win her happiness. A sadness rushed upon Indira, and she spilled her tea.

"There's more in the pot downstairs," Namrita said.

Namrita held the tea tray by her side, between thumb and forefinger, as she stood before them, drinking from her cup. For Indira, this casualness suddenly looked like cheerful hopefulness.

"Sit, Namrita, if you want," she said.

THE RAINDROPS FELL so fast on the bus roof that the clicking was like hail. It was the first rain. Prasad Kumar awakened and pulled himself up straight in his seat. The monsoon had been delayed again and again, until even August had appeared likely to pass without relief. He pushed open the bus window a little. Because there were no trees in the Old Vegetable Market, Prasad Kumar wondered whether the sweetness he smelled might be coming from the concrete of the buildings along the road. Within minutes, summer was gone. The plastic of the seat did not burn. It was possible to look into the sky without squinting.

As the bus moved slowly through traffic, clumps of naked boys began to appear on the sidewalk. Women with loose hair came out, and could be seen standing around, talking. And old men who believed in the healing powers of the first rain began climbing onto the roofs one by one. They were dark against a dark sky.

At the bus stand, the passengers got off slowly in newfound ease. The puddles on the road looked as if they were simmering. Prasad Kumar decided that he would buy samosas on his way home, and his family would eat them together and drink tea. He was glad to be returning home instead of going to work. Since the wedding, three months earlier, he had found himself wanting to be home more often. When he was out in the world, he felt as if there were too much of himself.

Soon after the bus started, there was a commotion in the back. A twelve-year-old boy was trying to get on without paying. The conductor was hunched over, his arms wrapped around the boy, who then lurched backward and dropped to the floor, slipping from the conductor's grip. Within a few seconds, the boy had crawled to the middle of the bus. He was wearing blue shorts and a dirty white shirt that was too big for him.

As the boy got up, he began to sing. He stood confidently, with one hand in his pocket, swaying a little with the motion of the bus.

He sang without appearing to pay attention to the song, but his voice was so steady, emotional, and intelligent that Prasad

Kumar was startled. He himself had once been a very good singer, and this almost forgotten talent had remained one of the secret sources of his own sense of himself. Meeting someone else who could sing as he had sung made him uneasy.

The boy's first song was well-known. It was about a saint who had gone on a fast to persuade God to end a drought and had died as the rains started. In the boy's mouth, the saint seemed to have a pride that Prasad Kumar had never noticed before.

"Here," a young woman said, and held out a two-rupee note to the boy. The boy started an Amitabh Bachchan song about all the fat, short, tall, thin wives a man could have and what it meant for his happiness. The song was famous from the movies, and went over even better than the one about the saint. This time several passengers held up money for the boy and tried talking to him in a friendly way when he came around to collect it. He only said thank you.

"For every song I now sing, I want fifty rupees," the boy then announced. Prasad Kumar had never heard a street performer make such a demand.

"A heart is such a heavy thing that we're always looking to give it away," the boy sang sweetly, and Prasad Kumar closed his eyes to listen. Ever since Arun got married and got his new job, Prasad Kumar's life had changed: parts of what he had always imagined to be his fixed nature seemed to be leaving him. He had not been drunk in months. He was rarely angry. Now that he had completed one of his great responsibilities—marrying off his elder son—he had begun to see that his final task of protecting Suresh would not be impossible. Or perhaps he just felt old.

For the first song, the boy gathered sixty-eight rupees. For the next, he received fifty-four. But for the third he got only forty-one. Prasad Kumar wondered if he was going to show some contempt for his audience.

"Thank you," the boy said, grinning. He then went to the front steps of the bus and stood there without looking back. When his stop came, the boy turned and shouted "Goodbye!" and then got off.

On the sidewalk, he walked with purpose, as if he were going somewhere in particular. The bus started, and the boy was out of sight.

Prasad Kumar bought samosas on his way home. In the flat, Arun and Namrita were reading a magazine together. Suresh was doing his homework. While Indira made tea, Prasad Kumar climbed onto the roof and stood in the rain like the rest of the old men.

YOU ARE HAPPY?

"Break her arms, break her legs," Lakshman's grandmother would say about his mother, "then see how she crawls to her bottle." What she said made sense. Lakshman's father refused to beat her, though. "This is America. I will go to jail and you will be sitting in India eating warm pakoras." To Lakshman, his father seemed unmanly for not taking charge.

Every time they went to a party, it was the same thing.

Before they left the house, his father would wipe down his comb. He would tuck a handkerchief into his pants pocket. He would get out the notebook in which he kept the lyrics of movie songs because he liked to sing and hoped somebody would ask him to.

The parties were segregated: there was the kitchen where the women gathered and there was the living room where the men stood and talked about politics, investments. His mother was thirty-two, short, stocky, curly haired. She would stir up trouble. Even the way she said ordinary things sounded doubting. "You are happy?" she would say to a woman, as if the woman were overlooking something. The surprised person would then feel she had to explain her happiness. The other women in the kitchen were not used to this kind of behavior. They would grow quiet and look at her and his mother would stand silently, appearing pleased, and take a sip of scotch. The fact that his mother drank was also unusual. Perhaps she did it to be different from the other women, perhaps it was to be like a man and therefore more important. When she had gotten a little bit drunk, she would go into the living room. She would stand among the men and drink from a small glass and talk about stocks and the World Bank. The men looked at her with condescension and irritation, not so much because she was a woman but because she was a woman and pretending to know things she did not, and vanity and foolishness that were tolerable in a man were not tolerable in a woman.

Lakshman's mother had begun drinking when he was eight. This was around when they were sent to America by his father's family, to grow the family's export business. From the very start, she behaved differently with alcohol than other people. At most parties, tea and juice were offered first and alcohol was an afterthought. At his parents' parties, his mother was the one who offered drinks. She pressed liquor on whoever entered the house. "Whiskey, bourbon, wine," she would say, smoothing each word. "Tea, Coca-Cola is also there." Sometimes the men they had over would praise her for her drinking or talk about their own, how it was with the third drink that they began to get happy. Whenever a man praised his mother for her drinking, Lakshman became anxious. Because of movies, he experienced a sense of sexual danger seeing his drunk mother talking to a man. Instead of joining the children in the basement, boys and girls his age who were delighted to be allowed to stay up late and who were running and playing and shrieking, he would follow her around the house. Watching her made him feel safer but also kept him anxious. By the end of the night he would be so exhausted he wanted to cry.

The drinking overtook her quickly. Around the time he was nine, she was drinking during dinner. His father, who rarely drank himself, protested. "Every night you have to drink?"

"I can't have a little happiness? Is there something wrong with me that I must suffer?"

And when he was eleven she started drinking during the day. His parents' marriage had been arranged because their families did business together; they had never shown each other any personal warmth. To the extent they spoke, it was either in shouts or in sarcasm. "Do you know what kind of people drink during the day?" his father said, shaking a finger at her. "Drunkards. You are a drunkard."

Lakshman, coming home from school, would sniff the air near his mother to confirm what he could tell with his eyes. If she was drunk, she seemed hollow, like she was directing her body from afar.

His family's life seemed strange to Lakshman, his father

shouting at his mother periodically but mostly ignoring her, often refusing to be with her, getting up from the kitchen table and leaving the room when she came in.

WHEN HE WAS THIRTEEN and about to graduate eighth grade and enter high school, his mother's kidneys began hurting. He would come home and she would be standing in the kitchen, holding a pack of ice against her side. Her caring so little about herself seemed to show that she cared nothing at all for him or his father. He would want to mock her and shout at her, but he was afraid she would hit him.

His mother did occasionally try to change. Once she went to a doctor and though she probably lied about how much she drank, the doctor still urged her to go to Alcoholics Anonymous. She went to AA meetings for a week or two and stopped.

In the past, Lakshman's father had traveled to India four or five times a year. As Lakshman's mother's drinking worsened, he began going more often. When his father was in India, Lakshman felt strange being alone with his mother, sitting at the kitchen table, doing his homework while his mother drank upstairs. The silence in the house was so intense it hummed.

When Lakshman was fourteen and his father was in India on one of his business trips, his mother decided she was going to stay in bed and drink.

Her room was large and had a cream-colored carpet. The bed was king-size, there was a picture window behind it and, to the side of the room, another window that looked onto a neighbor's roof and driveway. His mother appeared cheerful as she moved around the room. She opened the windows completely, although it was winter. She put two cases of wine on the carpeted floor beside the bed. Lakshman stood in the doorway and watched his mother's preparations. She put several jugs of water on the carpet also and, right next to the head of the bed, a large white plastic bucket to vomit in.

"Daddy won't like this," Lakshman murmured.

"Let him die," she replied happily. She put several large bags of potato chips on the nightstand. Lakshman, watching his mother, felt that what she was planning was so bizarre that it could not possibly happen. With the windows open, the room quickly became icy. His mother got under the quilt and picked up a glass of white wine.

Lakshman telephoned India. He gripped the phone and spoke in a soft tight voice. "Mommy says she is going to stay in bed and drink." Speaking, he knew his father would find some way of denying what was happening. His father said, "What else does she do anyway?" At his father turning what he had said into a joke, Lakshman got scared. He repeated what was going on, that his mother had gotten into bed and had been drinking for twenty-four hours. He felt detached from himself, like when he was taking a difficult math test and he was frightened but his pencil appeared to move on its own, hopping over the sheet of paper, jotting numbers.

His father didn't answer his reiteration. Lakshman knew the silence meant his father could later pretend what he had said had not been said. He repeated himself a third time. "What can be done?" his father answered in irritation.

For her first day or two in bed, Lakshman's mother sipped from a wineglass and ate potato chips and smiled confusedly at the TV playing in a corner. When she had to, she got up and stumbled to the bathroom at the end of the hall near his father's room. After a few days, though, she began shitting and pissing in the bucket.

Four or five days after she started drinking, Lakshman's father, forced to come back because of Lakshman's calls, stood in the bedroom doorway and screamed, "Die! At last there is nothing else." He shouted this, but he also phoned the county's central AA office.

Two women came to the front door of the house and rang the bell. One was blonde and short and looked to be in her early twenties. The other was much older and had very white, dusty-looking skin. Lakshman's father, unshaven, exhausted from the eleven hours' flight from Delhi, and so confused that he had a slipper on one foot while the other was bare, asked them to come in. Before entering, the women stood on the cement steps in front of the open door and prayed. They held hands and bowed their heads.

The older woman walked in first. As she passed Lakshman and his father, she mentioned that she liked Indian food. They went up the stairs. His mother's room was at the end of the hall and its white wooden door was closed.

They pushed it open and the room was freezing and full of light. To Lakshman, strained and desperate, the light seemed inhuman, as if they were above the clouds where it wasn't possible to survive. There was this light and there was the stench. The smell of vomit, urine, and shit was such that it did not seem thinkable that a human being ate there, slept there.

"You want to go to a detox?" the older woman asked Lakshman's mother. His mother was half sitting with her head against the headboard. She appeared stupefied. On her chin and down the front of her purple kameez were strings of dried vomit. It was embarrassing to have a stranger see his mother this way. Also, he felt a thin eager hope that these two women could fix her, that they were capable of doing something simple that would suddenly make everything all right.

The young woman picked up the bucket. Leaning to one side, she passed Lakshman and his father by the doorway and took it down the hall to the bathroom.

"If you don't go to a detox, you are going to die," the older woman said. She was speaking loudly and clearly.

The two women helped his mother stand. They held her from both sides and walked her down the hall. She was not wearing the pajama bottom of the long shirt and to see her yellow hairy legs was strangely awful. In the bathroom, she stepped into the tub with her kameez still on.

The women had come in a blue minivan and they drove her in it to the detox. Lakshman and his father followed in the family's Toyota with Lakshman clutching his mother's passport and insurance card. He wondered what a detox looked like. He imagined it resembling a grand bank.

It was a bright Sunday morning. They took surface roads so

the two vehicles wouldn't lose track of each other. The stores they passed were closed and their glass windows flashed sun. Lakshman began to feel relieved. The flashes of light were like blasts of music. The occasional person walking across a road seemed like life going on, like life was always going to go on and so somewhere there was the possibility of things being different and happiness existing.

IN INDIA, ON FARMS, pretty young women are as common as rabbits. It is easy to have sex with girls who are fifteen, sixteen, seventeen. These girls have nothing to trade other than sex and physical labor and often they are raped. On farms, when a girl goes alone into the fields in the early morning to defecate, there is a strong chance she might get assaulted.

Lakshman had been going back to India every summer since he came to America. When he did, he would go with his uncles to the farm that his father's family owned. He liked the farm, throwing rocks into a field and grasshoppers shooting up by the dozens. He liked the stepwell, walking down it to take a bath, the temperature dropping, the air getting sweet, and then squatting at the bottom step, splashing a bucket in the water to clear the tadpoles and weeds and beginning to soap himself.

On the farm, each uncle had his favorite girl. The girls would bring his uncles tea in the morning and disappear into their rooms for a half hour or more. Almost always only the men from the family went to the farm. A few times a year, for religious events that required visiting particular temples, the women of the family also came. These aunts and daughters screamed at the girls, chased them with sticks, and the farm girls urinated in the buckets of water used to wash the family temples. Lakshman did not think much about this. It seemed to him funny, like a television sitcom.

One summer evening when he was still fourteen, after his mother had gone to the detox and come back and started drinking again, Lakshman was standing by a sugarcane press near an irrigation channel. A girl who might have been nineteen came up to him. She was tall for a villager and barefoot, with a long skirt that had fingernail-sized, silver bells sewn on. Attaching a *jí* to his name as though he were the older one, she asked him in their regional dialect what months it rained in America. She asked this almost as if she had already heard the answer and wanted to confirm that she wasn't being lied to. "Every month," Lakshman said. "Every month it rains."

"Does ice fall too?"

"In winter."

"I had heard that," the girl said mysteriously, and then stood there for a moment as if she wanted to be remembered. She had a beautiful oval face and small breasts, and she appeared very confident.

The next day the girl came up to Lakshman again. This time it was early morning and he was in a field and his father's oldest brother, bald and with a mustache, was standing nearby chewing a tooth-cleaning twig. She thrust a little knotted rag into Lakshman's hand. "Some sweets," she said, and stared at him again. "How many air conditioners does your house have?"

"Run, girl," his uncle said quietly. "There is nobody here for you."

LATER, LAKSHMAN WOULD think that it was probably falling in love with this girl that caused his father to decide to have Lakshman's mother murdered. There was no other change to explain the events. His mother was no different from how she had been for years—drunk, quietly drunk sometimes, alarmingly erratic others. Once recently, his father had locked her in the bathroom when she was drunk and she broke all the mirrors. There must have been something about falling in love that made his father think that happiness was possible, that life was short, and that he should not stay with this woman who appeared to care nothing about anyone.

At the time, though, all Lakshman knew was that something had changed for his father. His father's room was next to his own. Sometimes Lakshman would wake at two or three in the morning from hearing his father on the phone. His father would be laughing in a happy relaxed way and when he spoke, he used their regional dialect. His uncles gave their girls phones and Lakshman guessed his father had done the same. Now, during the day, his father was more relaxed. The anger that had begun to live beneath his voice vanished. This was a relief, but it also felt like a betrayal. One fall afternoon when everything smelled wet, Lakshman came home from school and had to turn on the kitchen lights despite it being four. The house was quiet except for the soft sound of the TV in his mother's room where she was probably drinking. He saw that the answering machine light was blinking red. He pressed play and there it was, the young woman's voice. "Listen," she said in their dialect, and then there was some splashing. "That is my feet in water." She laughed and the phone hung up. Lakshman was furious. It was vulgar for her to leave a message. And she was a farm girl. She should know her place. He deleted the message. As soon as he did, he became scared his father would find out.

THE WAY AN ALCOHOLIC woman's murder gets arranged is that her husband sends her to her parents and tells them she is a drunk and not to be trusted and that he does not want her back. As long as he does not do this, as long as she is under his protection, she won't be killed, because she belongs to his family and not her father's. But once she is returned, her family will kill her, because the shame of having an alcoholic as a daughter or sister is staggering. It is even worse than having a daughter who is promiscuous. With a promiscuous woman you know to kill her right away, while with an alcoholic, the shame lasts longer because you hesitate.

Lakshman did not understand what was going on other than that his father seemed to be in love with a farm girl and was complaining more than normal. He started calling Lakshman's grandmother: "What kind of life is this?" he would ask. "What did you do to me when you got me a wife like this?" Afterward, Lakshman came to understand that his grandmother had to be consulted because, since his mother belonged to a family with which his father's family did business, there would be financial consequences if his mother was killed.

He sensed that there was a crisis building. His mother rarely went to India. Nobody wanted her there and so she only went if a close relative was getting married and even then only for a week or two. But now his other grandmother, the one on his mother's side, began calling, too. She wheedled Lakshman's mother, pressing her to visit even though there was no wedding coming up.

It was strange to hear his grandmother's voice on the phone. "Baby boy, go get your mother," she would say when he picked up. There were so many calls that it was obvious that something was occurring. The fact that his mother did not see it made her seem addled and helpless.

Talking to her mother, Lakshman's mother got giddy. Sometimes, after a call, she would stay downstairs and eat regular food instead of going back to her room and drinking wine and eating potato chips. Lakshman would then get nostalgic for the time she used to only drink at parties.

ABOUT TWO MONTHS after his grandmother began calling, his mother left for India. Three days after she left, barely enough time to land in Delhi, take the plane to Jaipur, and unpack, Lakshman was standing behind the stove making tea when his father came into the kitchen and said, "Your mother has died of dengue. She died in a hospital last night."

Lakshman felt he must be dreaming. He didn't turn off the stove as tradition would require after a death. Instead he continued making tea. His father stared at him. He had a round dark face and he stared at Lakshman nervously, as if waiting to see if he would be believed.

"Your mother died last night," his father repeated.

"In reality?" Lakshman asked.

"Yes. In reality." His father opened the refrigerator and got out a carton of eggs.

Lakshman felt a sense of relief. The sensation was like coming into a room that had been crowded with furniture but is now empty. The space seems smaller and like any other space, but also less stressful. He did not feel sadness, at first, because a part of him did not believe his mother was dead. If she were dead, he thought, they wouldn't be preparing food. It would be improper to do so.

He went to school. He did not tell anyone what his father had said. After classes, he attended track practice. Running in the cold moist air, he remembered when his mother had come back from her first detox, the one that the two women from AA had taken her to. She had been gone for four weeks. She had returned home at eleven in the morning and that afternoon she and he and his father had gone for a walk. Their street did not have sidewalks and so they had walked on the road itself, the snow squeaking beneath them, the trees in the yards dark from moisture. "Manuji," his mother had said to his father with a bashful half smile. "I am not going to drink. I don't know why, but I am certain." Her eyes were inwardly focused, as if she was looking at something within that comforted her and gave her confidence. His father listened but did not speak. He walked with his head down and he appeared frustrated, like somebody who knew he was being lied to and yet could not protest the lie.

He remembered this and remembered when his mother had had two black eyes because she had fallen down the stairs. The black eyes had made her look vulnerable and helpless and young. He remembered also when his mother had taken his father around the house and shown him where she had hidden bottles of alcohol. She had stood watching as his father put the bottles in a trash can and she had held her hands in the air and shaken them as if they were on fire and she was trying to put them out. Lakshman ran and tears slid down his face.

That night he lay awake listening but his father did not talk on the phone to his lover. The next night he did, quietly. And the third night, he was laughing like he always was. Lakshman felt revolted by him.

Weeks passed. The door to his mother's room remained closed. They told no one of her death. By this time in America they had stopped socializing, and so people only knew them tangentially and there were few to tell. Finally his father informed an acquaintance or two and somehow the news got to school. There Lakshman was pulled out of class by his guidance counselor and asked how he was doing. Talking to a white person in authority was frightening and Lakshman quietly said he was fine.

After perhaps a month, his father opened the door to Lakshman's mother's room. All the linens and clothes were, following tradition, going to be thrown away. Lakshman stood in his mother's room as his father opened the drawers and dumped the red, gold, peacock saris in black garbage bags. "I miss Ma," Lakshman said.

"You should. She was your mother." His father studied him for a moment before returning to work.

"Do you miss her?"

"Of course."

Later, the garbage bags sat slumped at the end of the driveway. It rained before the garbagemen came and the creases on the bags filled with water.

WHEN LAKSHMAN WENT to India the summer after his mother's death, his father's family complained regularly about not receiving help from his mother's relatives. He still did not understand that his mother had been murdered, and to him, his mother's family no longer helping meant a fraying of relations and it made him feel again that his mother was dead.

"Just because Aarti is gone shouldn't mean the relationship is finished," his grandmother said. "These relationships go from generation to generation."

"What can one do with a family that raises a drunk?" his father's second-oldest brother, skinny and with a scraggly beard, answered. "They are all crazy."

"They are not so crazy when it comes to their own interests," his grandmother spat back in the weird conspiratorial way she sometimes spoke.

Often these conversations occurred in the afternoon, after the family woke from its midday nap. They would all be groggy and irritable and the complaints would be like the bitterness in their mouths.

For a while Lakshman's uncle, the second-oldest brother, tried hinting what had happened. "They are scary people. Nobody owns seventy trucks without committing crimes."

Late in the summer, Lakshman realized what his uncle was suggesting. But his grandmother and uncle often said strange accusatory things, like that the local milkman diluted his milk with water and one time there had been a fish in the milk. It was hard, therefore, to take what his uncle said seriously.

"Who dies from dengue after one day?" his uncle insisted one afternoon.

"Keep quiet, idiot," Lakshman's grandmother said.

Besides, when Lakshman had arrived in Jaipur at the start of summer and visited his mother's family, his grandmother on that side had grabbed him and hugged him tight and sobbed. He could recall exactly his grandmother's arms around him, the boniness of her chest, the sharpness of her arms. All this seemed to cut through any of his uncle's hinted accusations.

But slowly, as the weeks passed and the monsoon came and people ran laughing through the streets and then God Krishna's birthday came, Lakshman began to feel a nervousness overtake him. He started having a hard time sleeping at night. The street dogs barking at two or three in the morning would wake him and he would become wild with panic. His grandmother sighing as she made her way to the toilet through the darkened house would pitch him into misery.

He went to the farm as he always did. There were gypsies passing through the area and at night there were puppet shows and men singing before the main house. In the morning there were the girls visiting his uncles. Once, he was walking through a field and he thought he saw the girl his father loved sitting beneath a tree talking to another girl. He walked toward her in the shimmering heat. As he did, the girl got up quickly and hurried away. Later that day, he asked the farm manager about the girl and the man said he would have her called. Lakshman told the man no and rushed back to the house. As he did, as he crossed the burnt grass, sadness filled him. It seemed awful that his mother had died, that his father seemed to have forgotten her, that this woman was still living her life.

That night, he couldn't sleep at all. He sat up in bed and the crickets were screaming and he thought of his mother and how on her nightstand she would sometimes have books from AA, how when she was going into a detox, she would become frightened at being away from home and would start crying, how for a while she had phoned the old white woman with the dusty skin who had taken her to the first detox, and his mother would stand in the backyard and speak urgently into a phone.

Around four the crows started cawing, and soon the smaller birds were chattering, as if they had dreams they were eager to share. At five the girls arrived on the veranda, slipping out of their rubber slippers on the steps, the slippers making a scratching sound as they slid onto the cement, then their bare feet going past his room, and the teacups they were bringing rattling on their saucers. Lakshman sat and listened and had the certainty that he could never come back to the farm again, that whatever happened he could never come back.

THE WELL

We lived frugally. If somebody was coming to the house, my mother moved the plastic gallon jugs of milk to the front of the refrigerator and filled the other shelves with vegetables from the crisper. The only meal my mother did not cook herself was our Saturday lunch. For this, my father walked six or seven blocks to get us slices of pizza. One Saturday morning, my father went to see a man who had recently come back from India with pickles and letters for his acquaintances, the way people used to do in the seventies. My father came home with a jar of mango pickles, but without the greasy paper bag from the pizza parlor. He took off his shoes and lay down on the bed with a cup of tea and the newspaper. When my mother went into the bedroom and asked if he was hungry, I heard my father say he had already eaten. My mother said nothing, only stepped out of the bedroom and closed the door behind her. After an hour, my father emerged from his nap and began to move around the apartment. Every time he came into a room my mother was in, she would get up and leave. Finally, my father demanded to know what ghost had stuffed itself into her. She started to cry. "I am just a servant. It doesn't matter what I feel. You would like it if I cut out my tongue and threw it away."

My father hurried from the house to get the pizza. When he returned, my mother refused to eat her slice. We were in the living room with its TV and plastic folding chairs, but none of us sat down. My parents stood there facing each other, and I stood between them. I began hopping in place. "I'll eat it," I chanted. I imagined myself from the outside, as if we were on a TV show and people were laughing at my cuteness.

"You have shown your heart," my mother scolded my father. "What else is there to say?"

"I'll eat it," I sang.

"Uma, are you a little girl?"

"My head hurts now. I can't eat."

"I'll eat it," I continued.

"Uma."

"I'll eat it."

My father turned to me. "You'll eat it?" he demanded.

I became afraid. I felt that if I did not go on hopping and acting cute, it would mean admitting that I was not like a boy on a show, that I was pretending and so I would reveal that I was dishonest. I nodded.

He smashed the slice into my face.

We stood quietly for a moment.

My mother took me to the bathroom and leaned me over the sink.

IN THOSE DAYS, I was always falling in love. I fell in love with Mrs. Muir from *The Ghost and Mrs. Muir*, with Mary Jane, Spider-Man's girlfriend, with Wonder Woman. I loved the last two especially.

I would imagine going for drives with Lynda Carter or for walks in a park. I imagined us sitting on a sofa and holding hands. The fact that I could not drive and Wonder Woman would have to drive for us embarrassed me. It made obvious the difference in our ages. I felt that the proper relationship for me was with Mary Jane, who was younger and a cartoon, although I liked Lynda Carter more.

Years passed. We moved from Queens to New Jersey. I was thirteen and the town we moved to had a lot of construction going on. When a house was nearly done, it would stand with landscaping around it, but one could see through the front windows into the backyard. If, on my father's evening walks, he came to a house with a new lawn that had freshly laid rectangles of turf, he would hurry home, get into his car, and drive back to the house. He would crawl over the lawn, peeling sections of turf from the yard. He would carry these into the back of his car and bring them home to our own lawn, which was yellow and sunburnt with rectangular patches of bright green.

One summer evening, I was sitting at my desk, in my room

upstairs, when I heard my father's car. In the back were the sheets of turf. My mother came running out of the house and stood by the driver's side door. "If you are going to steal, don't steal during the day," she screamed. "Do you know nothing?"

"Grass doesn't belong to anyone," my father said, getting out of the car. "Grass is like air."

"Do people pay to put air on their lawn?" My mother was so angry she was panting.

I cranked open my window. I leaned out. "Are you circus folk?" I yelled.

THEN, TOO, I OFTEN thought I was in love. First there was a girl named Joanne, who was very skinny and had square blonde hair and who worked at a dry cleaner. In high school, there was a pudgy girl with pasty skin named Cathy. Both were quiet and listened intently in class. Both were good at math and hoped to be engineers. Although I spoke to them only a few times, in each case I thought about the girl all day and dreamt of her at night. I would fantasize about living happily together and being good. When I am married, I thought, I will give my wife a single flower every day. In my fantasies, we were always married, although this idea was vague to me, represented mainly by our living in a house that had a dining table.

I went to Rutgers for college. I was fat. I didn't know much about women. My father once told me, "Pavan, don't be proud. Marry someone taller than you."

My mother laughed with malice. "The first well that gives this boy water, he will build his house next to."

After college, I started working as an accountant in the comptroller's office of a big pharmaceutical company. I liked working. I liked going to an office and getting a salary. I liked driving into an office park with lush green plantings and a fountain. I felt that I had been allowed into an important world. It was here that I met my first true love.

Betsy had short blonde hair and was thirty-one and very pretty. She had green eyes and her hair curled over her forehead. Sometimes a patch of it on the side of her head would stick up, and then she reminded me of Tintin. There was a scar on her right thigh where a malignant melanoma had been removed. And she played tennis, which made her seem more white than the other whites in the office. Betsy also flirted with all the men. If any of them had been away on vacation, she would greet him with a tight hug. The men in the office resented her, because she had gone out with a professional baseball player. The women disliked her, too.

For me, Betsy's beauty and her whiteness were hard to separate. I had only slept with one person till then, a very fat Hispanic girl. When I had lain on top of her, her belly had lifted me up and her face had been several inches below mine. I had penetrated her, but in the jerkings of my climax I had flicked out and had come on her bedsheets.

On Friday evenings, most of us went from the office to a bar. In the bar, I would try to be useful to Betsy and ferry drinks for her. I would stand near her among the other men and notice how long she spoke with each and what she said. I also regularly had lunch with her in the cafeteria. Often we talked about dieting. I would raise the subject because I felt the need to make my body real before her, to show that I, too, had a body. Also, Betsy was proud of her slenderness and liked talking about what she did to be so thin: having only coffee for breakfast and rinsing her mouth immediately so her teeth remained white, eating lettuce leaves with mustard for dinner several nights in a row if she knew she would be going out to a restaurant later in the week.

Often, I believed Betsy was beginning to like me. She would come by my cubicle at different times of the day or smile broadly when I went to her office. Then I would see her smile the same way at someone else and my heart would sink.

When Betsy drank too much on Friday nights, I drove her home. Many of the other men offered, but I think she felt safer with me. This belief of hers, that she was safe with me, made me angry. It was because I was Indian, I told myself, it was because she did not see me as a man.

One Friday night in December, perhaps because she had not eaten anything all day, she got very drunk. I held her by the bicep as we left the T.G.I. Friday's. "Be careful," I said, as we stepped off the curb. It was one of those cold nights when sounds seem loud and hard. We got to her apartment building and along the edges of the parking lot were snowbanks shining blue in the moonlight. "Let me walk you to your apartment." My mouth was dry. "It's icy."

The apartment was dark and smelled of ginger, and there

was a ticking sound. As she stood there, in the dark of her open kitchen, I tried to kiss her. "No," she said, and swung her head away. But I tried again, and she did not step back. This seemed promising to me. I kept my hands on her waist and kissed her cheeks, her ears. I remembered when my mother would hold both my wrists in one hand and slap me and I would try to duck and her hand would strike my brow, my eyes, the side of my nose. After a minute or two, Betsy put her hands on my face and kissed me in the practiced way of a woman trying to make a man feel desired. Now I became nervous. I felt that I had forced the situation into being.

"Should I go home?" I asked.

"Yes."

After this night, we kissed regularly, but only after she had been drinking. I would drive her to her building and say that perhaps I should walk her to her apartment, and my mouth would grow dry as we walked.

Kissing her was wonderful. To stand for an hour in her dark apartment, kissing, swaying side to side, made me so happy that I wanted to tell someone. In the car, driving back to my apartment, I would speak out loud to myself. "Is there anything better than kissing a beautiful woman?" I would say. "If there is, God is keeping it for himself."

At least once or twice a month we went to her apartment and kissed. There were occasions, though, when for several weeks in a row she would have dates on Friday night. I would feel very sad. My arms and legs would grow heavy, and I would find myself blinking away tears. I felt sad and also I would hate her.

Although I was the one chasing Betsy, I felt that she was using me, that to her I was simply a source of attention.

One day in the pantry at work, I came up to her as she was making tea in the microwave. "I would like to take you out on a date sometime," I said. I murmured this.

Betsy looked at me. She didn't say anything, then she patted my cheek and left.

On a sunny Saturday in spring, I was driving down U.S. 1 toward my parents' and I saw a blue Corolla like the one Betsy drove. I began following the car. I knew it probably wasn't hers, but every time I lost sight of the car, my heart began to race. "This is stupid. This is crazy," I said to myself, and the words spoken aloud made me feel my helplessness even more. I followed the car for an hour, until I lost it near the exit for Cranbury.

The weeks and months kept passing. I tried to distract myself. I would go to see my parents. My mother had lost a tooth near the top center of her mouth. The gap made her appear young. She remained mean, though. One of my high school classmates had become an investment banker, and she had learned from his mother what he earned. At the kitchen table, she asked me how much I made, even though she already knew. I thought periodically of telling her about Betsy, but I knew she looked forward to the prospect of negotiating my marriage, and she would get angry and perhaps start cursing me and Betsy if I told her.

BETSY AND I began having sex. I always tried to do it without a condom. She was still going on dates with other men, and I believed that if I could get her pregnant she would stop. Sometimes she demanded I wear a condom, sometimes not. Once, in the middle of sex, as she was on her knees and I was inside her, I, full of sexual excitement, asked what she wanted. "A rubber," she said angrily.

Despite the fact that we were having sex, I thought she did not care for me, that she was probably just tolerating me. I think, though, that she did care for me. I don't think it is possible to have sex with someone regularly without caring for the person. Once she told me I was the best lover she had ever had. I don't know what this meant. She sometimes spoke of a French soccer player she had dated as being the great love of her life. I asked her one night if she had told any of her friends about me. She said no.

Betsy was afraid of getting pregnant. For some reason having to do with her skin cancer, she couldn't go on the pill. Twice she had had abortions, once because of a rape. Occasionally after we had sex, she would lie there in the dark murmuring to herself, "I am pregnant. I can tell." She looked small and helpless then, her hair damp, sticking to her forehead. I couldn't understand why she would have sex with me without a condom. The only possible explanation was that there was something in her that was weak and baffled, just like there was in me. The sympathy I felt seeing her lie there, in the dark, murmuring to herself, would briefly brush aside my insanity. I would have the sense that I should leave this poor woman alone.

BETSY GOT PREGNANT.

"I want to marry you," I immediately said. We were both in her kitchen, in jogging shorts. I had imagined this day coming, and my saying this.

"I knew I shouldn't have told you."

"I love you."

As I told her I loved her, I felt, as I often did with Betsy, that what I was saying was a lie, a melodrama, a way to capture her, that things would not work out, that I was being foolish, that I was acting as if I didn't understand the reality of the situation, except that I did and was willing to break things and make things very bad just so I could get her.

Tears slid down her cheeks.

"Why are you this way?" she asked.

Seeing her pain, I was thrilled to be sharing an important moment with her.

"I love you. I want to marry you," I said, as if it explained everything.

Betsy turned around and walked away. After a moment, I followed her into her bedroom. She pulled her sports bra over her head, pushed down her shorts, and pulled back the sheets of her neatly made bed. She lay down on her left side, holding a pillow against her stomach, and closed her eyes. I didn't know what to do. I sat on the bottom corner of the bed.

After a while Betsy began to breathe deeply and evenly.

I got into my car to go home. As I drove, I was scared. I felt that Betsy would leave me. I also felt that our relationship was hollow, that it should end, that it consisted of my pretending various things and of her being bullied by my pretense into various halfhearted agreements.

I thought of going to my mother and telling her that I wanted to marry Betsy, that she had to come with me and make a formal traditional offer. I thought that if I did this, if I took my mother and did the things that are done when a match is proposed, I would be acting like someone who had behaved honorably. I would be showing that I meant what I said.

I took the Metropark exit and went to my parents' house.

My mother tilted her head to the side and stared at me. Sun was coming through the kitchen window. She had just bathed and her curly black hair was dampening the top of her green blouse. "Will you come with me to talk to her?" I said, my voice squeaking. "I love her." The Hindi word for love sounded silly outside the movies.

"Will you come today?" I asked.

"What is the hurry?" she said quietly.

"There is a hurry."

My mother stared at me. "Did you put something in her stomach?"

I didn't answer.

"She's educated," I said. "She's from a good family. Her parents are still married."

"Boy or a girl? You know?"

"No."

She sighed. "Boy or girl, both are family."

This was the first time I had thought of what was inside Betsy as a baby, as a child, as a member of my family.

My mother and I left for Iselin to go to the Indian jewelry stores. It was evening and the sky was darkening, and where the Indian shops start on Oak Tree, there was a banner above the road and traffic began to get very slow as men and women led their children across the middle of the street, looking at the cars and holding up their palms to signal stop.

In the car, I phoned Betsy. It was strange to call her with my mother present. "It's me," I whispered on her answering machine, and I thought about the baby inside of her. The poor thing was not loved the way a baby should be loved.

"She won't kill the baby, will she?" my mother asked. Many of my female cousins had been forced to undergo abortions when they learned their first child was a girl: to my mother an abortion seemed an unmediated cruelty.

"I don't know."

Inside the jewelry store, amid the crowd created by the mirrored walls, my mother and I sat on stools and looked at jewelry sets.

"What kind of earrings does she like?" my mother asked.

"Light ones. She says her earlobes are delicate."

"Does she like rubies or emeralds?"

"Emeralds. And she likes things she can look at more. Rings or bracelets more than earrings or necklaces." It surprised me to realize I knew these details about her. I felt a surge of grief because I knew my relationship with Betsy was probably going to end. I wanted to tell my mother details about Betsy. Both of her parents had worked, and for dinner Betsy and her sister would heat hot dogs for themselves. Her mom would call hot dogs "tube steaks." Betsy liked to do laundry and fold clothes but not to vacuum. If she had to choose between tennis and swimming, she would choose swimming.

Betsy agreed to meet with us—me and my mother. We sat on her white sofa in the living room, and she placed a tray of tea and cookies on the coffee table. When I had called her to ask if I could see her, she had said, "I am so angry," and her voice had been hard. "You didn't behave like a good man. I should have done something to take care of myself, but you didn't act like a good person." Now, she was polite. She told my mother how nice it was to meet her.

My mother put the red box with the jewelry on the table. She opened it to show the gold necklace and the earrings and the bracelets on the red velvet. "Daughter, I hope you will hear our request to marry Pavan. He will be a good husband. He is loyal and hardworking."

Betsy looked at the jewelry once and then back up to my mom. "Mrs. Mishra, I am not ready to get married. I like Pavan, but I don't want to marry him."

My mother was silent for a moment. "Daughter, will you consider marrying him?"

Betsy looked at us. "I don't wish to get married," she said softly.

"What he did was not respectful. It was not kind. But good

things can come from things that start badly. God is there in everything. He is there in the good and the bad."

"I will think, Mrs. Mishra, about what you have said."

My mother was silent for a while, then, in an almost pleading voice, she said, "Daughter, the baby is part of our family. It is part of your family, too."

BETSY DID NOT WANT ME to come with her to the doctor. I called her several times the day of the appointment, but it was dark out before she finally answered the phone. "It went fine," she said. "I'm just tired. I'm going to sleep."

My parents and I held the funeral ceremony for the baby on a weekday morning at the Sri Ram temple near Princeton. We sat in a far corner, hidden by pillars. There were only a few people in the temple. We had picked a weekday morning so nobody would ask what we were doing.

I sat across from the pandit. There was a fire between us, and he directed me to cut a ball of dough with a string and feed various stones by touching them with drops of milk. I was wearing a suit and it was uncomfortable there on the floor. My parents sat behind me watching.

"What is the baby's name?" the pandit asked.

I didn't know how to answer and I was silent, then my mother spoke. "We hadn't given it a name."

I started crying at how selfish I had been. I had been cruel and indifferent and had learned nothing from my own life. I put my hands over my face.

"It's all right," the pandit said. "We will call it Baby."

Later, in the car, I drove and my father sat in the front passenger seat and my mother sat behind me. We were on Route 27 when my mother reached over my shoulder and slapped me, hard. Her hand hit my face and ear. Her breath was loud. She reached over and hit me again. I thought, Good, I should be hit.

ACKNOWLEDGMENTS

This book would not have been possible without the support of the Dorothy and Lewis B. Cullman Center, the John Simon Guggenheim Memorial Foundation, and the George A. and Eliza Gardner Howard Foundation. Without these foundations a very difficult task might have been impossible.

I would like to acknowledge my gratitude for my employer, Rutgers University–Newark, which has given me time off to let me finish this collection. I also want to thank my wonderful and supportive colleagues in the English department and creative writing program. Ray Isle was the primary reader for most of these stories. His gift as an editor is almost supernatural. Lorin Stein also helped with these stories. I am glad that he told me to abandon two out of the three stories I sent him.

Jill Bialosky, my editor at Norton, has been my champion

since the very beginning. There could be no better house than Norton.

Lee Brackstone, my editor at Faber, acquired the first book I ever wrote and has been endlessly patient. I remember the first time I walked past the Faber offices (long before I had written a book) and felt deep hatred toward the company because I felt so small compared to Faber's history. How strange to be published by them now.

Last but not least, I want to thank my agent Bill Clegg. He has helped me in many ways, of which selling my writings is only one.

Also by Akhil Sharma

ff

Winner of the PEN/Hemingway Award

AN OBEDIENT FATHER

Ram Karan, a corrupt official in the Physical Education Department of the Delhi school system, lives in one of the city's slums with his widowed daughter and eight-year-old granddaughter. Bumbling, ironical, sad, Ram is a man corroded by a guilty secret. *An Obedient Father* takes the reader to an India that is both far away and real – into the mind of a character as tormented, funny and ambiguous as one of Dostoevsky's anti-heroes.

'The compassion and energy of Sharma's fine novel alerts us to this: a man is more than his crime.' Hilary Mantel, *New York Review of Books*

'Sharma's prose crackles with immediacy, shimmers with sensuality . . . Ram Karan may be a monstrous man . . . but, when it comes to his environment, his author gifts him with the eyes of a poet.' *Financial Times*

'A subtly rendered, marvelously detailed tragicomedy of contemporary India by an enormously gifted young writer.' Joyce Carol Oates

ff

Winner of the Folio Prize and the
International Dublin Literary Award

FAMILY LIFE

For eight-year-old Ajay and his older brother Birju, life in Dehli in the late 1970s follows a comfortable, predictable routine: bathing on the roof, queuing for milk, playing cricket in the street. Yet, everything changes when their father finds a job in America – a land of carpets and elevators, swimsuits and hot water on tap. Life is exciting for the two brothers as they adjust to prosperity, girls and 24-hour TV, until one hot, sultry day when everything falls apart. Darkly comic, *Family Life* is a story of a boy torn between duty and survival amid the ruins of everything he once knew.

'Outstanding . . . on love, duty, family, and what it means to become American. Every page is alive and surprising, proof of his huge, unique talent.' David Sedaris

'Deeply unnerving and gorgeously tender at its core . . . *Family Life* is devastating as it reveals how love becomes warped and jagged and even seemingly vanishes in the midst of huge grief . . . Beautiful.' *New York Times Book Review*